Copyright © 2013/2021 by Jannette Quackenbush

21 Crows Dusk to Dawn Publishing

ISBN-10 : 1940087082

ISBN-13 : 978-1940087085

This is a work of fiction. Names, characters, places and incidents either are the product of the author's imagination or are used fictitiously, and any resemblance to any actual persons, living or dead, events, or locales is entirely coincidental. This book was printed in the United States of America.

Table of Contents

Cuyahoga County

Delaware County

Gallia County

Greene County

Hardin County

Hocking County

Knox County

Lake County

Lawrence County

Logan County

Lorain County

Lucas County

Madison County

Montgomery County

Morgan County

Muskingum County

Pickaway County

Pike County

Preble County

Richland County

Allen County

State Hospital Cemetery
The Grave of Celia Rose
E Chapman and Bible Road
Lima, Ohio 45801
40.773666, -84.094852

The Ghost of Celia Rose

The grave of Celia Rose.

Celia Rose.

In 1896, 23-year old Celia Rose fell in love with a neighbor boy who did not return her affections. Understanding that their daughter only had the intellectual ability of a small child, when Celia began to hound the young man for affection, her mother and father sat her down and firmly forbade she visit him again.

Angry, Celia added the poison Rough on Rats to their morning cottage cheese and killed her mother, father, and brother. Celia was found guilty in court, but the judge acquitted the young woman for mental illness. Instead, authorities sent Celia to Lima State Hospital in Allen County, where she died in 1934. She was buried in the state hospital cemetery. Those traveling past the old cemetery have seen an older woman walking among the graves and recognize her as Celia Rose.

Auglaize County

Old Ohio and Erie Canal
County Highway 182
St Marys, Ohio 45885
40.617862,-84.352863

Bloody Bridge

An early boat on the canal.

During the mid-1800s, passenger packets and cargo boats traveled the man-made waterway of the Miami and Erie Canal from Toledo to Cincinnati. A driver guided a mule that walked the towpath along the shore and pulled the boat. During the time of the canal, in the area between Spencerville and St. Marys, there were two boats commonly seen along the waterway—the Daisy and the Minnie Warren. Jack Billings was a big, softhearted man and a driver for the Daisy. A moody man by the name of William Jones led the mules for the Minnie Warren. The captain's daughter was on board this boat, and it was her name given to the packet. She cooked for those on board and rode faithfully by her father's side on the canal route.

Boat on the canal.

Minnie and Jack would often flirt playfully with each other as their boats passed. After some time, they both realized they loved each other. Jack found himself counting the hours between the time Minnie's boat disappeared after passing and when he would see it appear in the distance again. Minnie felt her heart pound wildly when she shyly caught the man's eyes in hers while they teased each other whose boat was the better. All of this flirting made William Jones quite jealous as he loved Minnie too. He would have mentioned his liking to the young woman, but he knew she only had eyes for Jack Billings. It would not have made a difference anyway. So he just seethed over their fledgling relationship from sunup to sundown. He tossed and turned at night, dreaming up ways to get the girl all to himself.

The Miami Erie Canal where the story played out and the two young lovers would see one another.

It was not until one evening in the fall of 1854 when William's jealousy peaked after a social event both Minnie and Jack attended. Late in the evening, as they walked home along the canal, they paused at the bridge. Little did they know William was waiting for them in the shadows with a sharp-edged ax. In one stroke, the bitter man cut Jack down. Minnie fell backward over the edge of the bridge and into the water below. She drowned in the murky waters of the canal. Some would say it was shock that sent her reeling to her death, but others believed the moment Jack died, she did not want to live at all and took the plunge to be with him in the end.

The original wooden Bloody Bridge is long gone, but the legends surrounding this section of the canal still remain.

Not long after, someone stumbled upon the gruesome scene of Jack's lifeless body and saw the girl floating dead in the water. They brought her body up and laid it next to the bloody one of her sweetheart. Gone, they were. But each of the young lovers left their mark on the region. For nearly forty years after Jack's body was removed from the bridge, the bloodstains left from his body remained engraved in the wood. And hence, it received its name—Bloody Bridge.

Those who looked over the edge of the bridge where Minnie died said they would see her face staring up at them from beneath the muddy canal water.

Historical marker by bridge.

Fort Amanda State Park
22782-22798 Ohio 198
Lima, Ohio 45806
40.684544, -84.269818

Ghost Cabin

Fort Amanda—where some have been startled by a unique type of ghost.

In the early 1800s, American trade and the ability to gain new territories were restricted by the British to the point a war began in 1812. During this time, a series of forts were erected from Piqua to Perrysburg as supply depots and staging areas where troops and equipment were readied for military operations.

Fort Amanda rendition.

Fort Amanda was one of these fortifications constructed on the west bank of the Auglaize River. Rafts were then built to transport soldiers and supplies downriver. When it was abandoned around 1815, settlers moved into the safety of its walls. Many years would pass, the fort was left to decay, and all that remained was a cemetery of soldiers and settlers. Finally, a monument was erected, and the property became a park. It was about this time that people began seeing a mysterious image of a cabin or blockhouse appear with lights flickering in windows after a sudden rain shower. As they stepped forward to take in the incredible sight, it faded away.

Butler County

Old Commercial Building on High Street
241 High Street
Hamilton, Ohio 45011
39.399459,-84.560587

When the Ghosts Haunted Ryan's Tavern

When it was Ryan's Tavern.

For quite some time, three buildings on High Street made up Ryan's Tavern, and workers often spoke of the haunting there. A kitchen worker, Kizzy, saw shadows while she worked and heard ghostly voices. She told the manager, Tully Milders, that things moved on their own. Kizzy would get the supplies ready for a recipe and lay them out randomly, leave the room, and return to find the items in perfect order to begin cooking.

The kitchen where ghostly Elizabeth helped workers.

Kizzy fondly nicknamed her ghostly helper, Elizabeth. Tully was intrigued by Kizzy's story. He started looking deeper into the history. He talked to a local one day, and the man mentioned that Jonson Brothers Confectioners was once located in the building. They had two ladies who worked in the kitchen making the candies. One of them was named *Elizabeth*!

Doug, the morning cook at the time, headed to the basement one day and loaded a cart. The cart slid across the concrete floor not once but at least four times while he stared in disbelief.

Missus Irene C. Shoupe, a music teacher, ran the Shoupe Music School in part of the building from 1922 through 1967 while her husband Stanley was proprietor and director of The Music Box, a music store. Stanley passed away in 1953, but occasionally he still visits—some have heard music after closing.

Tully Milders and my son at the haunted elevator.

Tully was always light-hearted about the ghosts, "They help me out almost every morning," he would often say. They were helpful at times. When he would bring in an armload of boxes after the morning truck delivery driver dropped them at the back door, the elevator would open as if a ghostly hand pressed the button to welcome him inside.

Bridge Over Tracks on Maud Hughes Road
Liberty Township, Ohio 45044
39.394545,-84.410448

Screaming Bridge

The Screaming Bridge.

Not far along Maud Hughes Road, in an area once quite isolated but now dotted with homes, there is an overpass above train tracks called Screaming Bridge. Here, the dreadful sound of screams are heard by those driving across the bridge, and a phantom train rolls along the still-used railroad beneath. Most attribute the strange occurrence to the many railway accidents occurring over the years in the region, and one in particular not too far away.

On a cool October day in 1909, Engineer Charles Wikoff hitched a ride to his home in Middletown on a Big Four fast train engineered by Oscar Pease. The train would have been heading past this section of railway if the boiler had not exploded about a mile above Gano Station en-route to its destination. When it burst, both men were scalded to death, their screams echoing in the air. Some believe the train will forever run this route trying to take Wikoff home. And the screams of the dying men are carried with it.

Rose Hill Cemetery and Hamilton-Princeton Road
2421 Hamilton Princeton Road
Hamilton, Ohio 45011
39.388929,-84.526856

Vanishing Hitchhiker

Rose Hill Cemetery off Hamilton-Princeton Road where some believe a ghostly hitchhiker resides.

A young woman wearing a 1950s blouse, poodle skirt, and saddle shoes hitchhikes along Hamilton-Princeton Road. Occasionally, someone picks her up, but she vanishes as the car passes Rose Hill Cemetery.

Champaign County

Old Railway Tracks in Urbana
Ohio Bicycle Route 3
Urbana, Ohio 43078
40.114926, -83.751634

Lincoln Ghost Train

The train that carried the body of Abraham Lincoln across the United States has been seen as a phantom train complete with ghostly, pale faces staring out the windows. *Image: Library of Congress*

Do not forget to mark April 29th on your calendar as the date the nine-car Lincoln ghost train wanders down the same tracks in Urbana that the actual train took on the same day in 1865. One week after President Lincoln's assassination on April 14th, 1865, the funeral train carrying his body weaved its way across the northern United States on its route toward Springfield, Illinois for burial. It made frequent stops along the way.

And it was not merely to allow mourners to pay respects to the late president along the 13-day trip. There were layovers often to freshen the flowers surrounding the corpse to keep the smell of rotting flesh to a minimum. As the train progressed along its route, one of the places it trudged through was Urbana on Saturday, April 29th at 10:40 p.m. Thousands showed up to see the train pass.

You can watch for the ghost train from the Simon Kenton Trail, a hike/bike path in Urbana. Public Parking for Trail Access: Depot Coffee House, 644 Miami St, Urbana, Ohio 43078 (40.109011, -83.759691)

Nowadays, a few folks show up for another reason. Legends say that on April 29th, a ghostly funeral car carrying the body of President Lincoln makes its way along the tracks through Urbana on this special anniversary date. Some have seen it shrouded in black with a skeletal crew within while others have simply seen ghostly lights that vanish into nothingness. Those with homes near the tracks have awakened to the sound of a ghostly train rambling along the railroad. The spectral scream of the whistle sweeps along the railway, and legends persist that clocks throughout town stop for 20 minutes, the same amount of time Lincoln's funeral train stopped in this pretty village.

Clark County

George Rogers Clark Park
Daniel Hertzler House
Museum
5072-5098 Lower Valley Pike,
Springfield, Ohio 45506
39.909216, -83.911192

Staring Out the Window

The Hertzler home.

Daniel Hertzler was an early Mennonite settler from Pennsylvania who prospered as a businessman in Clark County—including being the president of the Clark County Bank. Along with his wife, Catherine, and ten children, he built a small empire of a farm, sawmills, and even a brick distillery. Hertzler owned a large house on a property overlooking a village once belonging to native Shawnee, now the George Rogers Clark Park. The family was worth quite a bit for the times, and many believed Hertzler kept much of his cash at his home.

On a chilly October night in 1867, robbers came into 67-year-old Daniel Hertzler's home and took more than his money—they stole his life. It must have been a shocking surprise to be awakened by his wife, who had arisen to care for a sick child. She told him she heard a noise in one of the rooms. Only moments later, the surprised robbers would be making their way to Springfield with Hertzler's horse and buggy. Hertzler would be dead on the floor.

None of the men suspected of robbing Daniel Hertzler's home and murdering him faced prosecution. Police caught two suspicious characters, but they escaped. No one paid for the wicked deeds they had done. Hertzler was buried in Ferncliff Cemetery in Springfield beneath a tall monument bearing his name. It is quiet there, the birds sing soft songs in the summer, and the wind blows gently across the freshly mowed lawn. Not so in the place that Daniel Hertzler called home. His corpse might be in the quiet of the cemetery, but his spirit haunts his old house overlooking the Shawnee Village. Hertzler's face has been seen staring out the window, perhaps looking for the men who murdered him, waiting for their return so he can give them their due.

Springfield, Ohio 45502

The Ghost's Calling

In February of 1907 in Springfield, Daniel Clauer, a night watchman at the State Odd Fellows Home, fell from the top of a boiler and was killed. Not long after, his one-year-old niece, Maria, passed away quite suddenly. Daniel's 56-year-old wife Mary began to have visions of little Maria working her way toward her surrounded by angels, calling out to her, and beckoning the woman to follow. She told her family, who scoffed at the dreams. They thought that her visions were nothing more than imaginings due to her grief for her husband and Maria, whom she cherished so dearly. They thought it would surely pass with time. However, the visions continued for a month before Mary was found dead in her bed one morning, finally answering the ghost's calling.

Clinton County

**Wilmington College
College Hall**
*College Street
Wilmington, Ohio 45177
39.444827,-83.818229*

Old Bill

College Hall.

Quakers established Wilmington College in 1870, led by Civil War Colonel Azariah Doan. College Hall was the first building opened in 1871, offering a diversity of uses—from a dorm for faculty/staff to a public meeting place. It also housed the skeleton of Azariah Doan's beloved horse, Old Bill. Brought to the college after the Civil War, the horse became a big part of memorial ceremonies. After it died, the college displayed the entire skeleton for many years, but later, only the skull was left out to view. Students relate that the horse's ghost returns, and its hooves clomp along the hallways at night.

Crawford County

Banks of the Sandusky River
399 Aumiller Park Drive
Bucyrus, Ohio 44820
40.802375,-82.991588

Ethyl

Near the banks of the river.

Many years ago, a young woman named Ethyl Hanley who lived on a farm near Bucyrus, fell in love with a man ten years her senior. However, her father forbade the two from being wed until she had reached marriageable age. To help the time pass more quickly, her sweetheart would take Ethyl to pick flowers along the banks of the Sandusky River.

When it finally came time that the two could wed and two weeks before the vows were to be made, Ethyl was killed when thrown from a carriage. The sweetheart walked the banks for years, alone and wishing Ethyl would return. After some time, he came no more. Then passersby began seeing a young woman picking flowers along the same banks before suddenly vanishing.

Old Horace Burger Cottage
Young Road
Tiro, Ohio 44887

Suicide Grove

The Horace Burger Family. Photo Courtesy Joe Blum, Great grandson of George Burger, Horace's brother.

Horace Burger had a small cottage built in June of 1901 and placed on Baker Road in North Auburn by Fred Klinghardt, who had mysteriously vanished shortly after finishing the house. It was to be the new home of his newlywed daughter Emma and son-in-law Adam. They moved in during the autumn of 1902, even though Klinghardt was found dead by his own hand beneath a tree in the grove next to the cottage in October 1901.

The haunted cottage. The Bucyrus Evening Telegraph February 16, 1903 Aesculapius, Correspondent

The young couple should have been ideally content, but immediately upon moving into their cozy home, at night, there were mysterious tappings on the windows and doors. As soon as they laid their heads down upon their pillows, moans and groans would seep up from seemingly nowhere, disturbing any sleep they would try to get. At first, Emma and Adam believed they were a target of a practical joke by friends. But within a few weeks, the couple began seeing a bent figure wandering around the woods near the cabin. Soon after, though Adam locked the doors each night and he firmly secured the windows, a strange light would appear within the house, along with a mungy, damp scent. Then, shortly after weary sighing groans, the figure would reveal itself within the cabin, meandering aimlessly from room to room.

The couple prepared to leave the cabin. However, Horace Burger refused to believe a ghost haunted the building. So one night, he stayed in the cottage and made himself a bed for the night, fully expecting to sleep from dusk to dawn without being disturbed. Or, if it was a neighborhood prankster, he would quickly stop the shenanigans for good. No sooner had Burger fallen to sleep when midnight came, he was awakened by a cold breath against his cheek. He bolted upright and peered into the darkness, recognizing the form of Klinghardt. Burger immediately went to the task of ridding the ghost by snatching up a stick by the fireplace and tossing it right at the apparition. The piece of wood went right through the misty form. He lit a lamp, but the ghost had vanished.

"SUICIDE GROVE."

A correspondent for The Bucyrus Evening Telegraph took this shot of the Suicide Grove where Klinghardt died. He wrote that if you looked just to the left of the center of the image, you can see the ghost.

Sure that he had waylaid the ghost, Burger made himself comfortable in the bed only to be awakened once again by the form rambling around the house. The man picked up his belongings and went home. Of course, when he told the story, some laughed and set out to prove the man wrong. But one by one, each saw the ghost. The local Doctor Miller and a journalist were even more relentless. When each visited, they brought a camera to the home. After strolling to the woods and the hanging tree, they took pictures with a camera. When the pictures were made available, the ghost of Fred Klinghardt appeared. Then in 1903, the ghost vanished.

**Brownella Cottage
& Galion Historical Museum**
132 South Union Street
Galion, Ohio 44833
40.73373,-82.7912

The Giving Ghost

Brownella Cottage is haunted by previous owners.

There is an old house in Galion that Ella and William Brown owned. For some time, William was the reverend at Grace Church in Galion and later, Bishop of Arkansas until his unusual views of economic and church structure did not conform with the Episcopal Church.

The couple haunts Brownella Cottage. Although most remember William as the bishop who was ousted by the church for his strange beliefs, others would recall the couple purchasing truckloads of food for the poor during the Depression and William standing in his yard and passing out nickels to schoolchildren on the sidewalk. Perhaps William would like people to remember him for the latter, and that is why passersby have seen his ghost tarrying near that same sidewalk.

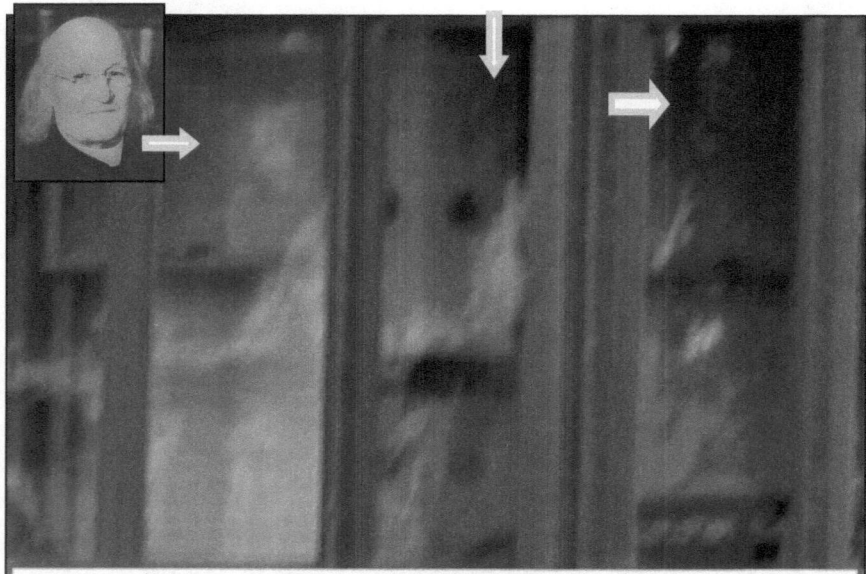

I took lots of pictures when I visited Brownella Cottage. Several came back with ghostly images and above is one. If you look at the window pane to the left, you can clearly make out the image of the aged William Brown. In the center pane, there appears to be a woman, perhaps his wife. And the pane to the right offers a younger version of Brown in church robes waving or giving a blessing!

Cuyahoga County

Erie Street Cemetery
2254 East 9th Street
Cleveland, Ohio 44115
41.497039,-81.683654

Joc-O-Sot

Erie Cemetery is Cleveland's oldest public cemetery. Before the land for it was purchased, an impromptu lot on the N.E. corner of Ontario and Prospect was used. But as the city crept up on its gates, those within were moved to the Erie Cemetery grounds.
Photo Courtesy: Michael L. Sekeres.

Erie Street Cemetery holds early settlers in its grasp, along with two American Indians. One haunts the grounds—Joc-O-Sot, a chief of the Sauk. Although he fought against the U.S. in the Black Hawk War, he later became a fishing guide along the lakeshore.

Joc-O-Sot died in 1844 at age 34 and wanted his remains taken to the northern part of the U.S. He is one of the ghosts roaming the cemetery, a little angry about getting trapped in Cleveland for eternity. He is seen sometimes as a shadowy figure darting around. Legends tell that Joc-O-Sot was so furious that his burial was at Erie Street Cemetery, he made the earth shake, and his gravestone broke. A new marker replaces the old, but you can still see the shattered stone behind it.

Old Tiedemann Home
4308 Franklin Boulevard
Cleveland, Ohio 44113
41.485656,-81.716521
It is privately owned but can be
viewed from the street.

Franklin Castle

Franklin Castle.

In a mansion on Franklin Avenue in Cleveland, there was once a family named Tiedemann living there. They seemed to have more than their share of bad luck with childhood disease. Of their six offspring, only two lived to adulthood. Most of the infants died within ten years, along with 15-year-old Emma, who had diabetes.

Many years after the family had moved out, people living at the old home complained of shadowy figures and mists forming then vanishing. They even heard the sound of babies crying.

Delaware County

Old Robinson Place
Underneath the
O'Shaughnessy Reservoir
Delaware, Ohio 43015
40.18275,-83.12751

The Old Haunted House of Delaware

Road to the Haunted House, near Marysville, Ohio.

Along the Scioto River and just off a heavily traveled road and then a short dirt path, there was once an old haunted house. Little remained of it, but a skeleton of stone and brick, faded fresco paintings on its ceiling and walls, and a small tomb nearly hidden in the brush of the yard. People who traveled to see it would often feel a certain unease as they peered into its interior and took a sniff of the dusty air. Some of the bolder would light a lantern and enter and nearly get lost in its black depths of room upon room filled with shreds of peeling wallpaper, broken furnishings, and windows long gone of their glass.

Then in some dark corner, they might see a young woman, shaking and quivering while she squatted on the floor. As they blinked wildly at their find, she would fade a moment, reappearing in a bent position that made it look like she would dart off, that which she did. Finally, there would be a pitter-patter of feet, and she would vanish into the blackness. Some would bolt to the safety of the front door. Others searched her out, although they could never find her.

Remains of the home in the early 1900s.

In the late 1800s, many picnicked next to the old house. It was generally agreed by the romantic that the man who built it was an Englishman who had come to the isolated area in 1834. He had knocked upon the farmer's door who owned the property and stated he wanted to buy a piece of his land near the river. Not expecting the outsider to buy it, the farmer, not used to strangers, set an exorbitantly high price on the property. However, upon producing the amount in Spanish gold coins, the farmer could not disagree that the land would be perfect for this strange man.

Those in the tiny community watched curiously as an enormous and extravagant home was built with tapestries and wallpaper and beautiful paintings on the ceilings. There were stairways and room upon room dressed with the finest furnishings. Once it appeared there could be nothing more added to the grand home, the man left for some time, then returned with a beautiful girl most believed was the Englishman's wife. He also brought several servants.

For many days, the man, girl, and servants lived reclusively within the home, keeping to themselves—no one living in the house went outside the property, and nobody in the neighborhood was invited within. It was not long, though, that those passing on the old rutted road by the house heard screams and cries when they passed by. But if they dared go near, the sounds would disappear as if someone was guarding the area and whoever made the pitiful sounds was hushed swiftly.

Along the Scioto River at O'Shaughnessy Reservoir where the home once stood.

One night, the farmer who had sold the property was returning home late from the local mill. He was somewhat surprised to come upon a group of horsemen riding toward him. Not knowing who they might be and thinking they could be thieves, he slipped into the brush and hid while they passed. However, as they went by, he could see that it was the Englishman and his servants, and between them, the young woman who was supposed to be the Englishman's wife was tied to her saddle, weeping and begging not to be killed. The farmer stayed quiet and was able to hide until they were gone, then made haste to his home.

However, the next night as the man was riding back after completing an errand, he saw the same group returning from somewhere unknown. The woman was not among them. As he tried to secret himself in the brush again, his horse tripped on a root, and he was thrown. The cluster of men quickly surrounded him, and through a series of questioning, found out what the farmer had seen the night before. Instead of killing him, they made him sign an oath of secrecy and gave him a leather sack of gold to seal the pact.

The stranger lived in the home for nearly twenty years. Then during a cool October, hunters found the house abandoned. The furnishings and those within were gone. It appeared the home was ransacked but tossed upon the floor were papers that revealed the Englishman had been a pirate. When he had amassed a great fortune, he retired and chose this place as his home. But only weeks before he left the seas, he had come upon a ship with a high-ranking Spanish family aboard. He killed them all but one beautiful child, a girl he sent to a French convent until she was sixteen. Then she was brought to the home along the Scioto River and lived and perhaps died by the pirate's hand.

Years would pass, and a happy family bought the home who left, saying a young Spanish woman haunted the place. Of course, nobody would stay there, and it was eventually abandoned and left to only picnickers who sowed the story of the pirate and his captive. And the ghost.

Gallia County

Chimney Rock
Wayne National Forest
Symmes Creek Road
Patriot, Ohio 45658
Parking: 38.81497, -82.45428
Trailhead: 38.815055, -82.455033

Chimney Rock Screamer

Chimney Rock. To find the trail, park just before the old bridge in the gravel pull-off. A small trail sign after the bridge (left side) of the road marks the trail.

Deep in the forest of Gallia County, there is a tall rock spire that locals call Chimney Rock. A woman committed suicide there, and not long after, her ghostly screams were heard by those passing on Symmes Creek Road nearby.

Greene County

Ye Olde Tavern
228 Xenia Avenue
Yellow Springs, Ohio 45387
39.805893,-83.888775

Woman in Blue

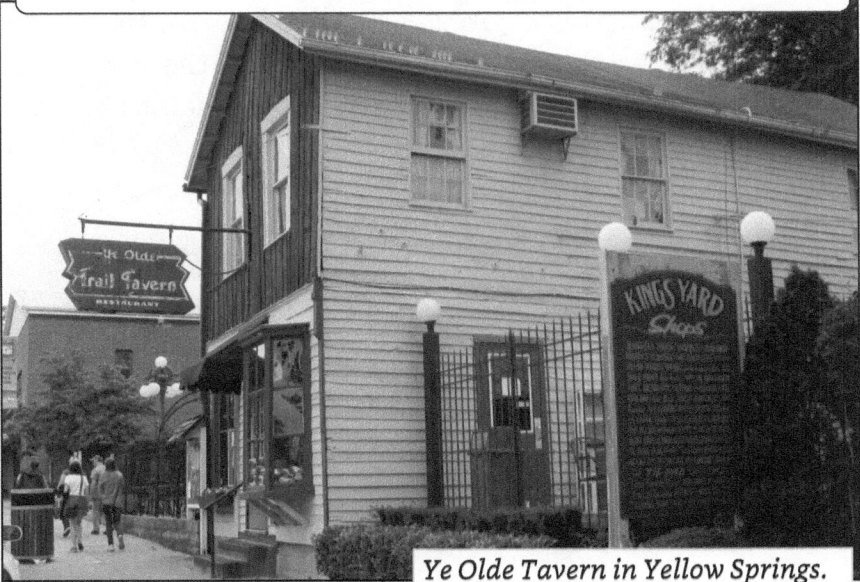

Ye Olde Tavern in Yellow Springs.

There is a ghost of a dark-haired woman wearing an 1800s blue dress who roams the hallways of Ye Olde Tavern in Yellow Springs. Her existence is explained like this— Frank Haffner owned a cabin in what was later Yellow Springs and along the old stagecoach road in 1844 and opened it as a bakery. When he died, he requested in his will that his wife Rebecca would not remarry. She lived 17 years after his death, never taking another husband. Now, she returns, lamenting her lonely life without another.

Frank Haffner had a son named Charlie, who inherited the bakery. He liked to pull pranks on people in the community. Charlie and a friend, Bock Shaw, talked another man called Johnny Kleen into snatching a body from the cemetery to sell to the doctors in Cincinnati for education for a whopping $25.00. Johnny would have to sneak into the graveyard, recover the body wrapped in a blanket, and take it to a conductor at the train station. Johnny Kleen did just that, except partway to the railroad depot, the body he was carrying reached out and grabbed him tight and said aloud: "Boo!" It was Bock Shaw beneath the blanket. Charlie Hafner said Johnny never stopped running until he was well out of sight. Charlie still plays jokes at Ye Olde Tavern. He moves benches, pushes chairs so that they fall to the floor, and sometimes startles folks by whispering their names in their ears!

Clifton Gorge State Nature Preserve
Yellow Springs, Ohio 45387
Parking off Jackson Street:
39.794942, -83.828476
Walk Gorge Trail less than a
mile to Blue Hole:
39.795109, -83.839102

Spirit of Blue Hole

Blue Hole at Clifton Gorge is about a mile walk with steps from the parking lot (1-way) along the Gorge Trail and beside the Little Miami River. You will see its deep pool not long after Steamboat Rock.

Long ago, there was an Indian woman whose tribe lived near the location of Clifton Gorge State Nature Preserve today. She was in love with a man from her tribe. However, he loved another. One afternoon as many of the young men and women gathered for an outing along the pretty valley where the Little Miami waters flow blue and deep, she watched as a rival flirted playfully with her love. The man she loved, he flirted in return.

It was as if he did not even notice that the infatuated woman existed at all! In a fit of jealousy, the young woman decided to force the man to see her and choose her over the rival. She would hurl herself from the wall to the waters below. He would certainly note her falling, turn his back on the flirting woman, and rush to save her. He would finally see she was much more beautiful than the others.

Thus, she clambered up to the highest rock, screamed into the air to catch his attention, then jumped. Instead of running to save her, the man turned to the young woman with whom he had been chatting and let his young admirer drown. Now, there are times when the evening turns its back to the day sky, and when the moon lights up the valley that you can see the young woman standing atop the rock. Her ghostly screams fill the air before she jumps and disappears into the blue waters below.

Trebein Road
Trebein Road
Fairborn, Ohio 45324

Ghostly Bride in a White Gown

The old road where a ghost walked—

In the late 1800s and on a cold winter night, a boy worked his way up an old road in his father's carriage returning home from a social event. His horse, an aged and trustworthy mare, made a slow, sleepy trod on the packed dirt. So dead broke was she that the boy had to jiggle the reins because otherwise, she would stop altogether and fall to sleep. And such, inconveniently, she was beginning to nod off as he came upon a lonely stretch of road with an old graveyard.

Before he caught sight of the graves, the horse came to a standstill and began to move rearward until she backed over a shallow ditch and rammed the carriage into the graveyard fence. The mare snorted, eyes rolling and sweat breaking out on her neck, and the boy's head wheeled around to see what was frightening her. Just within the confines of the graveyard, he could see a beautiful woman in a white dress. "Oh, come on!" she said in a hurried voice. After, she raised from the ground and floated over the graveyard fence and out into the road, stopping just feet from the terrified horse and boy. She began to walk, beckoning the boy to follow. It was too much for the mare. With a single swing of the head and a panicked snort, she burst from the fence, over the ditch, and out into the road, not stopping until she and the boy were at his family's barn.

A lonely stretch of road and the old cemetery along Byron Road—

In the mid-1800s, on the day of her wedding, a young woman was putting on the beautiful white dress her mother had passed down to her. As she tugged it over her waist, a seam came loose. Although the women who were helping her prepare for the ceremony quickly snatched up their needles and thread, repairing the hem, it was close to the time for the wedding to begin.

The bride-to-be hurriedly climbed into her father's wagon and urged him to get to the church quickly. "Oh, come on!" she cried as they started, urging her father to drive the horse faster. And so he did. But the old rugged road was muddy and filled with ruts and stones. Finally, when they came upon a straight stretch, and the horse was at a canter, one old worn wooden wagon wheel pitched upward on a rock and threw the young bride into the air. When she landed on the ground, her head hit the stone that had joggled the wagon, and it killed her instantly.

They buried the girl in a small church cemetery along Byron road. The father and the would-be groom shoved the rock to the side of the road and let it roll into the ditch where it can still be seen today, along with a ghostly bride in a white gown who walks Trebein Road at the location that her carriage ride came to a swift halt and at the graveyard where she was buried.

Hardin County

Ridgeway Cemetery
20569 Township Road 179
Ridgeway, Ohio 43345
40.524663,-83.553497

Anna Bell's Grave

Anna Bell Davis's grave.

We know little of Anna Bell Davis's life. She was born in 1862 and lived with her widowed mother, Nancy, and younger sister, Mary, at Bokes Creek. On October 15th, 1881, and at the tender age of 19, she died. The writing on her headstone reads: *Remember youth as you pass by, As you are now, so once was I. As I am now, so you must be, Prepare for death and follow me.* It is this eerie epitaph that draws people to her grave like an incantation summoning the living to their death. Her gravestone is said to feel warm to the touch.

Harden County Armory
128 North Main Street
Kenton, Ohio 43326
40.649086,-83.607708

Pranksters

The armory—

The Hardin County Armory in Kenton is haunted. Even in its early years, those within witnessed slamming doors, ghostly apparitions, ghoulish laughter, and the spectral sound of footsteps. Before the armory was built, the property was owned by a German grocer named Frederick Johns who had many children. Some believe it is his dead family members who come back to play pranks on the living there.

Hocking County

Scotts Creek Falls
13843 State Route 93
Logan, Ohio 43138
39.532216, -82.420650

The Death Hole

The Death Hole at Scotts Creek.

It was a Tuesday morning deep in the summer of 1887 when 29-year-old Johannes Bensonhafer loaded his wagon with twenty bushels of wheat to deliver to the local mill in Logan. Along with him was Johannes' new wife, 19-year-old Clara. They had been married a little shy of six months. Once settled into the wagon, the two traveled along what is now a part of State Route 93 but was then called Scotts Creek Road. At just about 10:25 a.m., they passed the ford along Scotts Creek and headed a little farther past a layer of stones called 'The Falls' along the left side of the road.

A man following in a carriage watched the couple pass the ford as he continued onward just a short way. Suddenly, he heard a loud clatter and the scream of horses forcing him to turn his carriage around. To his horror, he found the team of horses that had been pulling the Bensonhafer wagon struggling hard in a deep pool of water. Johannes and Clara had vanished, but a hat and basket were floating near the surface. Tiny bubbles gurgled from somewhere below.

For unknown reasons, Johannes had turned the wagon along a deep section of water that local legend held was a nearly bottomless passage beneath the falls called Death Hole. Most likely, the man driving the wagon had no clue a 12-foot drop lay hidden beneath the water. He had innocently urged his horses forward. They had plunged downward along with the cart laden with wheat. Clara and Johannes were pitched forward and tossed like ragdolls into the water.

The young couple and their team of horses were pulled too late from the water. They lay the corpses of Clara and Johannes on the bank, waiting for the coroner. It was not long before crowds came to see the dead couple lying there in a state that described them as seeming to appear as if they had fallen asleep on the bank, complete with rosy color still upon their cheeks.

The family buried the couple in nearby Ewing, and local newspapers would deem the tragedy the 'Awful Calamity at Scotts Creek.' Folks talked about the couple's sad demise for years. Then, that news faded away. But the Bensonhafers, do not rest. On some nights, you can hear the wagon along the road followed by muffled chatter of the young couple as their ghostly wagon slips toward the bank near the falls. Then there are the screams of horses as the phantom team descends into the murky depths of Scotts Creek and disappears.

Knox County

Kenyon College
Old Kenyon Residence Hall
204 College Park Street
Gambier, Ohio 43022
40.371579, -82.397292

Old Kenyon

"Old Kenyon", Kenyon College, Gambier, Ohio.

The first building was established at Kenyon College in 1827 and fondly dubbed Old Kenyon by those who stayed within its rooms. But in the early morning hours of February 27th, 1949, sparks from a fireplace cut into an old chimney. The embers slipped their way through a flue and into a space between the second and third floors. Within moments, the building went up into flames, leaving little more than a gutted shell appearing like a charred skeleton made of blackened bricks. Nine students died in the fire.

The school rebuilt over the old structure, and soon after, students inside would see the ghosts of the fire victims in misty forms sweeping down the hallways before vanishing.

Brink Haven (Brinkhaven)
South Main Street
Brink Haven, Ohio 43006
40.468280, -82.194921

The Fortune-teller

After the 1913 flood, Harry and Katie Workman's bodies were recovered at the head of the mill race at Brinkhaven with some help from a local fortune-teller. Image: Knox Times.

At the tail of March, 1913 severe winter rainstorms hit the Midwest, causing rivers to rise. Katie and Harry Workman were in their mid-twenties with a four-month-old child living on the west side of Brinkhaven close to the Thompson Mill and along the Mohican River. Harry was a telegrapher for the railroad, working late the night before.

Such neighbors believed the young couple was sleeping in late on that Tuesday morning that the river rushed through the town. Katie and Harry must have been rudely awakened by the crash of water forcibly hitting their home and the grate and grind of beams and wood while the waters beat it down. As the flood peaked, witnesses saw the couple jump from the house when it collapsed, and along with it, swept downstream.

When the waters of the Mohican began to recede, rescue workers from the town started searching for the Workman family, but for many days, found no clues of their whereabouts. Finally, after some time, Charles Workman, Harry's brother, despairing over the loss and desperate to find the couple and child, went to a local, but well-known, astrologer and fortune-teller named Ebenezer Gorham in nearby Newcastle. He asked the man if he knew where the couple and child could be found. Gorham pondered over the question, then made a brief statement saying that the bodies of Katie and Harry were at the head of the mill race, and the child named Glenna was downriver.

Charles Workman lost no time gathering people in the community to build a temporary stone dam to redirect the waters and then drain the mill race. The fortune-teller was right—beneath the surface, they discovered the bodies of Katie and Harry, dressed and clutching each other tightly. Unfortunately, the child's corpse must have headed downriver because it was never found.

Long-gone Fairchild Estate
The Maplehurst Mansion
Corner of Division and
Gambier
Mt Vernon, Ohio 43050
40.391751, -82.477158

The Maplehurst Mansion Ghost

The Maplehurst Mansion in Mt Vernon, now gone. A ghost, however, may remain.

On Saturday, April 22, 1905, 56-year-old Miranda Bricker was making her way toward Maplehurst Mansion on the corner of Division and East Gambier streets in Mt Vernon. It was the residence of the Fairchild family, but it was also where Miranda worked as a housemaid since the previous October. One of the perks of her employment at the home was receiving a room to stay.

She had been visiting her sister Jane earlier, and as it was Easter Sunday the next morning, she wished to retire early. It was a cool evening around nine o'clock and dark when she made her way to a gravel path that led from Division Street to her employer's door. Only moments after her shoe hit the gravel, an assailant sent a blow to the woman's face so hard that the force knocked her false teeth clean from her mouth. She cried out, "Oh, my God!"

A neighbor, Missus Swigert, heard the peculiar shout and ambled curiously over toward the yard. She peered about cautiously and spotted shadows moving in the dewy grass and noted a strange gurgling. However, she decided it was nothing more than drunks or tramps who had jumped off the train that night and were making their way through town. It would not be until the next morning that a maid working in the home gazed out a window and saw Miranda Bricker lying assaulted and dead in the grass.

The property where Maplehurst Mansion once stood is now occupied by condominiums.

Bloodhounds were brought in and followed the scent to a local quarry and then the home of a black man named George Copeland. Police were quick to arrest him, as was a mob who readied themselves to lynch him. Copeland was secreted out of town, denying that he killed her. Later, as there was no evidence tying him to the murder, he was set free. The police never found the killer. And old-timers talked for years of the ghost of a housemaid who used to stroll Division Street to the walkway of the mansion.

Lake County

Paines Hollow
The Old Lerman Farm
Paine Road
Painesville, Ohio 44077

The Well

The road at Paines Hollow.

Many years ago, in a place called Paines Hollow, there was a man named Frank Lerman who owned a farm. He had a handyman, Harry Lipenstick, who disappeared quite suddenly. Many knew the young man and asked where he had gone. Lerman only shrugged and told them Lipenstick had taken off for parts unknown. Several years would pass, and the farm went through several hands until it was eventually sold in the early 1920s to Carl Logies from Cleveland.

Not long after Logies moved into the home, he began seeing strange things. Night after night, as he headed to the barn at 9:30 p.m. to check his cattle, something white would float past the building and to an old well near the road. Logies knew the old well had been unusable as it was filled from bottom to top with stones and debris. But it piqued his interest, the strange white form, so he began to pull out the rocks and rubbish discarded within one day. About twenty feet down, he found an old, rotted shoe. Inside, there was a man's skeletal foot and toenails.

Immediately, Logies contacted the local sheriff, who had the well completely dug out, and inside was a decomposed corpse of a man. Amongst the bones, there was a watch that contained a rare ruby charm that townspeople knew belonged to Lipenstick. It had stopped at exactly 9:30 p.m. It was this watch that identified Frank Lerman as the killer. He was arrested and charged with the murder. And the ghost of Harry Lipenstick stopped floating past the barn and to the old well.

Rider's Inn
792 Mentor Avenue
Painesville, Ohio 44077
41.713052,-81.260119

Greetings from a Ghost

In the early 1800s, Rider's Inn was a stagecoach stop along the Buffalo, New York, and Cleveland route, first run by Joseph and Suzanne Rider. It is now an inn and restaurant. Long-dead Suzanne still greets guests with the same type of hospitality offered two hundred years ago and has been seen by those visiting at the front door and on the upper floors.

Willoughby Village Cemetery
Willoughby, Ohio 44094
41.63931, -81.41083

Girl in Blue

She came in on the last streetcar from Cleveland on the 23rd of December of 1933, the young woman who would later be known as the Girl in Blue in Willoughby. She was let out of the car at Kirtland for lack of money to pay the fare. A kind gentleman stopped her and inquired if she needed assistance. When she asked where she could find a room for the night, he walked with her to Mary Judd's boarding house on 3rd Street in Willoughby. He helped her make arrangements to stay.

After settling in about eight in the evening, she retired to her room. The next morning, Christmas Eve, she asked Missus Judd (who described the girl as quiet and wistful) how she could get to the train station to inquire about a ticket and where she could attend church. Missus Judd gave her directions for both, and off the girl went—in the wrong direction. Laughing, Missus Judd chased the girl down and waved her the right way. It would not be long before the young woman returned and, after wishing the older woman a Merry Christmas, clutched her purse and prepared to leave once again.

From the boarding house, the girl left along the street, eventually leading her past the cemetery. Then, she worked her way along 2nd Street toward the New York Central Railroad tracks. From there, she disappeared behind a grove of maple trees, possibly looking for a shortcut across the rows of train tracks to get to the other side. It was with a sudden urgency that she made a swift dart forward as if the young woman realized too late that the train was coming. And it was too late. The eastbound train heading to New York burst past, giving her a sidelong blow that pitched her body along the side of the tracks.

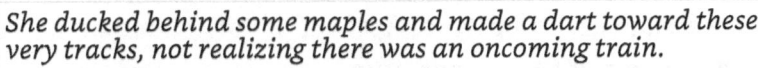
She ducked behind some maples and made a dart toward these very tracks, not realizing there was an oncoming train.

She died instantly from a fractured skull. When local authorities recovered the body, they found little on her person but ninety cents, a brush, some pencils, and blank envelopes—and, some say, a ticket to Corry, Pennsylvania. Yet there was nothing inside to show who she was or the direction from which she had come. They carried her body to the local funeral parlor owned by James McMahon. The identification of the body was this: She was five feet and four inches, weighed approximately 135 pounds, had red-brown hair, and hazel eyes. She had high cheekbones. She was wearing a blue woolen dress and a blue wool coat, floral scarf, and blue shoes. But the rest was a mystery.

After several days and the young woman's body was not claimed, authorities buried her in the Willoughby Village Cemetery in a bare plot within a simple casket. No headstone marked the life or death of the young woman who had passed so softly and ephemerally through the town of Willoughby. However, the mystery of her identity piqued the curiosity of those in the community and across the United States. Some with missing daughters sent letters to the city officials asking if she was their child.

Several people stepped forward, maintaining they recognized the Girl in Blue. In April of 1934, police believed the mystery was solved when two little sisters residing in a West Virginia orphanage saw pictures of the deceased and identified her as their 20-year-old sister, Mary Dalbaugh. However, Mary quickly contacted an aunt to show she was alive and well and working in Cumberland, Maryland. In May of 1934, a Mansfield resident, Budd Goodwin, misidentified the mysterious girl's effects as belonging to his wife, Elsie. Soon after, he received both a call from his wife and a handwritten letter stating the body was not hers at all.

But the girl was not forgotten. In April of 1936. Hank Heaverly, the cemetery sexton, had collected enough funds to provide a marker for the young woman with a discounted rate from a tombstone dealer. There was enough money left over to buy flowers for the grave. The headstone would state: IN MEMORY OF THE GIRL IN BLUE/ KILLED BY TRAIN/ DECEMBER 24, 1933/ 'Unknown but not forgotten.'

But within a month of funding the headstone and on the 14th of May, 1936, the Sandusky Register reported that the mystery of the Girl in Blue might be solved. Leo Klimczak, of suburban South Branch in Pennsylvania, was shown pictures of the mystery woman and identified her as his 21-year-old sister, Josephine, whose nickname was Sophie. She was the daughter of Polish immigrants, Jacob and Kathryn Klimczak, and had left her family's farm in Corry, Pennsylvania, along with her brother and headed to Detroit.

Like many young people during the Great Depression, the two were searching for jobs to help the family financially. However, neither could find work. Discouraged, they decided they had no choice but to abandon their search. They were barely able to scrape up enough money for return fare home for Sophie. And that is how she ended up heading in that direction and Willoughby nearly penniless and lost, trying to find her way home.

Sophie's ghost is lingering near her grave. You can visit it. It is in the Willoughby Village Cemetery. If you enter from the Sharpe Avenue entrance, drive past the first intersecting road and three trees. It will be on the left— tenderly cared for and tucked under a Mulberry tree along with another stone marking the grave in front of the old— *Girl in Blue. Identified as Josephine Klimczak. The 24th of December, 1933.*

Lawrence County

Woodland Cemetery
824 Lorain Street
Ironton, Ohio 45638
38.507274,-82.648602

Slapped Lady

Osa Wilson's grave.

Osa Wilson was the wife of a prominent businessmen in Ironton. She was married nearly seventeen years and a mother of six when she became ill with colitis and neuritis in 1911. She died one month later at the age of 33. Osa was buried in Woodland Cemetery, and legends stemmed from the lifelike statue that there is a handprint donning the left cheek, a sinister slap from her killer who knocked her down some stairs while she was pregnant, killing her. If you press your palm to her belly, there is a certain warmth emanating from the stone.

Lake Vesuvius Recreation Area
Wayne National Forest
Lake Vesuvius Road (CR 29)
Pedro, Ohio 45638
Furnace:
38.605356, -82.630159

The Devil Went Down to Vesuvius

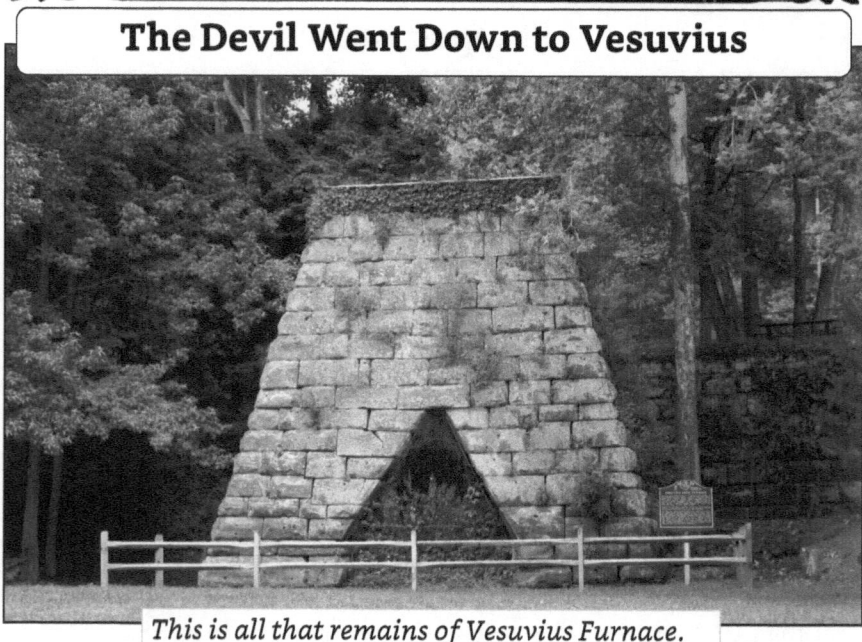

This is all that remains of Vesuvius Furnace.

In the 1870s, a man from Long Creek was riding his horse in the neighborhood of Vesuvius Furnace heading home. During this time, the furnace was still in operation. The road, although somewhat isolated, was typically busy at certain times of the day with laborers coming and going to work. However, as the rider came to a certain point, the workers had already dispersed to their job or home. He was quite alone.

As his horse came upon some brush on the side of the road, a strange creature with a thin body, low squatty legs, and a long black tail burst into the rider's path. The man pulled back on the reins, startled, but before he could come to a complete stop, the beast had disappeared. After a thorough search of the area, he could find nothing.

When he went to town the following day, he mentioned the strange creature. Others had seen it too, and most believed it was the Devil himself that had been burped up from the fiery depths of the furnace. For many days, this devil barred the path of riders and workers until a priest was called in to confront it. The priest met the Devil head-on, asking it, "What in the name of God do you want?" There was no answer. But the Devil disappeared and was not seen there again.

Logan County

Harrod Cemetery and Highway 56
4900 Township Highway 56
Bellefontaine, Ohio 43311
40.423173, -83.782884

Hatchet Man

Beware the Hatchet Man on this road. And when you pass Harrod Cemetery, watch for his unmarked grave that glows bright green.

Andrew Hellman was a tailor by trade, arriving in America from Germany in 1817. To most with whom he crossed paths, he was well-mannered, good-looking, and had a wealth of friends. He married Mary Abel— blithe, buxom, and light-hearted, and within a short amount of time, he had built up a business and a farm on what is now Township Highway 56 outside Huntsville. The couple had three children—two boys and a girl. One April morning of 1839 after his children had grown, Louisa (age 17), Henry (age 16), and John (age 12), awakened quite ill. Within a day, Louisa and John both died and were buried together in a single grave.

After her children's deaths, Mary recalled picking up a jug of milk, and upon seeing a powdery substance on it, she decided not to drink the liquid. It occurred to Mary that her son and daughter might have drank the milk and were poisoned. But she kept it to herself, only once mentioning her fears to a sister in a note. It was too horrendous a thought that the children's father, who was the only other person who had been in the home, would kill them. *Or fear.* Unbeknownst to all around them, Mary and the children had been suffering horribly at Andrew's hand.

The next month, Mary sent her only surviving son, Henry, to live with her brother, George. Several days would pass, and no one heard from Mary. George's wife went to check on her. She found Andrew Hellman alive and lying on the bed covered in blood and Mary's mutilated body lying on the floor, an ax slicing through her skull.

Andrew was questioned and jailed, but before his trial, he fled to Maryland, starting anew with a farm and changing his name to Adam Horn. Then he married a 16-year-old girl named Malinda. On a stormy, snowy night in March of 1843, Andrew Hellman murdered his second wife in cold blood. He dismembered her body and hid the parts throughout the farm in old coffee bags and a trunk. This time, when arrested for the murder, Andrew was convicted and executed for his crimes. He also was given the name of Hatchet Man from those who heard his story.

Nearly a thousand spectators came to watch him hang. His remaining son buried him in an unmarked grave in Harrod Cemetery along Township Highway 56. But just about as many have probably driven along this road passing the cemetery looking for his ghost. Some nights, his spirit runs along the street, a hatchet in his hand, waiting for some unknowing Samaritan to stop and give him a ride.

Lorain County

**Ruins of Swift Mansion -
Light and Hope Orphanage**
*52374 Gore Orphanage Road
Amherst, Ohio 44001
41.355052, -82.335234*

Gore Orphanage

The Swift Mansion—part of Light and Hope Orphanage aka 'Gore Orphanage' before it burned down.

There is a story about an orphanage in Lorain County. While the children who lived there were sleeping in their beds, Old Man Gore, who ran the place, nailed all their doors shut. Then, he lit a match, caught the place on fire. Inside, the children awakened to a fiery death, tiny fists pounding on the barred windows and doors. Then they all went up in flames.

Well, not *exactly*. There was an orphanage on this piece of land along Gore Road built from the Johnathon Swift Mansion and a few surrounding farms. It would become the home of the Wilber family for about thirty-five years. Later, it caught the eye of John Sprunger, wealthy industrialist/ builder, and his wife, Katie.

A capitalist at heart, Sprunger had founded the Light and Hope Missionary Society in 1893 along with the Light and Hope Orphanage. Around 1903, Sprunger had purchased the Hughes farm in Amherst along with three other neighboring farms, including the Howard's farm and buildings to house the children.

It was here the Sprungers established the printing shop and publishing company under the guise of an orphanage trade training center for children. Actually, the children, ranging from about seven to seventeen, were indentured servants—forced to do free work providing services in the printing company and working the farm. Sprunger also rented the children out for agricultural work as hired hands to surrounding farms.

His scheme was not new—children had been bought from Victorian workhouses and overworked without wages in exchange for board and food as pauper apprentices in England since the 17th century. To the public eye, he posed as a saint; his undertakings had all the appearances of a training facility where teachers taught boys a trade and girls learned domestic sciences. In reality, the children were victims of Sprunger's capitalist greed with the deceptive outward appearance of evangelism and charity. The boys lived at the Hughes farm, and the girls dwelt at the old Howard farm. The children's overseers lived at the Swift Mansion. The Light and Hope Orphanage encompassed over 500 acres.

A 1910 U.S. census shows 45 people were living on the property, including 27 children, Katie and John Sprunger, and fifteen helpers and assistants. But sources state there could have been 125 children on the property at a single time. The caretakers were not caregivers at all, but wardens/overseers for the laboring children. Sprunger treated children like slaves and got rich off their labors. From the onset, the complaints and investigations of abuse and slave labor at the farms plagued the orphanage. It came to a head in 1909 when children began to run away and tell local, empathetic Amherst townspeople about their abuse. It got so bad that nearby townspeople established an underground railroad for escaping children.

Beatings were a common form of punishment to the children by both overseers, the Sprungers, and local farmers when they worked. The Sprungers also forced their slave labor to eat spoiled food. Bedbugs, lice, and rats were commonplace in their cots at night. A sick cow found dead in a field was used for the children's meals. Instead of a doctor's care and medicines, they called upon prayer for healing. A litter of bunnies was strangled in front of the children by a teacher to threaten the boys and girls. The orphanage, by judge ruling, was placed into different hands.

So it was true that a cruel man ran the orphanage. There was also a fire when authorities investigated the orphanage over allegations of abuse—in 1910, a boxcar filled with oil and printing supplies burned. It was a three-story building completely destroyed used for the printing of the Sprunger's Light and Hope Magazine. It exploded so heartily that flames filled the sky. There is no mention in newspapers of children killed during the explosion or fire, nor is there mention that there was an investigation by local authorities held to check for foul play or deaths. Records of the number of children at the orphanage were poorly kept and rarely accurate.

Although the considerable fire that killed hundreds of children may not be confirmed, there are ghosts of its past and plenty of them. The orphanage stayed open until 1916. The old mansion was burned down in 1923 by some homeless taking up residence. People did die here—two of the initial owners, the Swift children, are buried in the Gore Orphanage/Andress family cemetery. There are probably a few settlers who died here in Ohio's early days. At least one little orphan boy was killed nearby, 'coasting' on the back of a car. And those old, disturbing memories still linger of cruelty on the property to sad little orphans who may have returned to the place to haunt Old Man Sprunger and his hired hands for their beatings and slavery.

The Swift Mansion—then.

The Swift Mansion—now.

A keen eye can make out the old horse hitching post..

There have been tales of a ghost child swinging on an old tree. And while carrying a recorder at Gore Orphanage, I heard a child's voice say softly, "Tryphenia."—that is how I found out about the Swift's children, researching what the word meant and finding it was the name of a daughter who died at age five in 1831 there.

It is worth the hike beneath the trees to search out the foundation, find the old well, imagine what it looked like before fire burned the mansion to the ground. Some put baby powder on the back of their car to see the tiny handprints show up. Try it. Maybe, you will see the ghost of someone's past like thousands before you. Because they say, they have.

Lucas County

Oliver House
27 Broadway Street
Toledo, Ohio 43604
41.643253,-83.538262

The Captain

The home of Maumee Bay Brewing Company, a restaurant, pub, and brewery, was once a historic hotel. During the Spanish-American War in 1898, the Oliver House was an infirmary for wounded soldiers. As a result, guests have seen a man dressed in full uniform appear before their eyes. They have fondly dubbed him 'The Captain.'

The Historic Commercial Building
301 River Road
Maumee, Ohio 43537
41.56434,-83.645942

The Dangling Ghost

There is an old building on River Road in Maumee built by Levi Beebe in the 1830s and called the Commercial Building. Among the many uses over the years, it was a public meeting room, bank, and mercantile business. However, old-timers would say that it was also used to harbor and convey alcohol during Prohibition. It was at this time that a woman hanged herself on the upper floor. After those passing through the room where she suicided would see her ghost dangling from a noose.

Wolcott House Museum
1035 River Road
Maumee, Ohio 43537
41.572359, -83.638714

Mischief-maker

Wolcott House Museum—

Back in the early 1820s, a local merchant named Wolcott built a house near the Maumee River. He married, and over the years, the couple had many children. A few generations later, the home became a museum complex. Someone from its past must have been quite a mischief-maker. Because mysterious things happened after the guides began giving historical tours.

Once, volunteers set up a Christmas display with mannequins, and whenever they left the room, workers would return to find the figures rearranged into different positions. Then there was the time a display case was carefully set up by cleaning staff. When they left the area and passed back a little later, the display was entirely repositioned!

The Fallen Timbers Battlefield and Fort Miamis National Historic Site and Trail
I-475 & US 24, 4949 N Jerome Rd, Maumee, Ohio 43537
41.549710, -83.699358

Death Dance at Battle of Fallen Timbers

In the evening and as a dark storm loomed on the horizon, I waited for a ghostly battle to play out. The old dead would not be able to entertain me that night as the tornado sirens began to wail and knowing the land's history, I went on my way to safety. But I bet even without me, the ghosts danced death that night—

During the late 1700s when Mad Anthony Wayne and his soldiers fought the Indians, there was a bloody clash called Battle of Fallen Timbers. In the area where it occurred and on stormy nights, those traveling past the site have seen what appears as a ghostly dance of death among soldiers while the old battle plays out.

Benjamin Joy Cemetery
4718 Brittany Road
Ottawa Hills, Ohio 43615
(Behind St. Michaels)
41.665617,-83.653601

One-legged Captain

Benjamin Joy Cemetery—

The freight captain of a ship in Lake Erie lost his leg in an accident while transporting a cargo of wheat. He bought a wooden pegleg, fit it over the remaining stump, and continued on with life quite happily. However, when he died, his family buried him without the pegleg. Reasonably discontent at the conquest of going through eternity unable to walk, he hops around the cemetery after death, searching for his missing wooden pegleg.

Somewhere off the Toledo Shores

Red Rover

A scow schooner.

In the late 1860s, Captain Patrick Shaughnessy of the boat Red Rover was killed. A Captain Connelly took the dead man's position and began sailing his scow schooner on the dangerous and shallow waters of Lake Erie near Toledo. One day while the boat was out in the waters of Lake Erie, it sprang a large enough leak that the ship was going to sink.

All hands on board quickly went to the pumps or the sails, and between the two parties only resting for short ten-minute periods, they began working on pumping the boat to move at a pace fast enough they could make it to shore without sinking. After many hours of grueling work, however, the men were exhausted. They began taking turns sleeping and working in shifts. When they were trading places for sleep, it came to be that nobody was at the pumps as they had all retired to their bunks and were in deep slumber. Nearly two hours passed without a single crew member pumping the water or handling the sails. The lake was tossing the vessel back and forth, and the crew was surely going to die in the sinking boat. But when the third hour passed, the captain was roused from his sleep by hands wrapping in his hair and dragging him from bunk to floor. He blindly made his way in the darkness of night to the bunks of his crewmen and awakened them with desperate shouts. They set about to see how much water was within the boat. But, to their amazement, there was none at all!

When the sailors finally returned to the safety of the shore, the captain asked his crew who had awakened him so desperately during the night. The men had stared at him, then looked from one to the other. No man stepped up to say they were the one to rouse the captain and save them all from certain death. If it was no one living, it must be someone dead. The men decided that it was Patrick Shaughnessy whose dead hands pumped the water that night while the crew and captain slept. And it was his ghost who awakened Captain Connelly in the darkness and dragged him from the bed. After that, the captain and crew deserted the scow and refused to work that boat again.

Madison County

Red Brick Tavern
*1700 Cumberland Road
(Route 40)
Lafayette, Ohio 43140
39.938304,-83.406515*

Blood Red

Built around 1836/1837 along the National Road halfway between Columbus and Springfield, it became the second oldest stagecoach stop in Ohio with 24 rooms for travelers. Six presidents have stopped there on their journeys. In its time, it acted as a private schoolhouse from 1854 to 1864 run by the Minter sisters (there were six of them) who lived there. The Red Brick Tavern has a ghost story to tell: One of the Minter girls became ill and committed suicide. Her spirit roams the second floor. An embroidered sampler she was making states *Remember Me.* It now sits in the second-floor hallway and is stained blood red due to her ghostly hands.

Montgomery County

Amber Rose Restaurant
1400 Valley Street
Dayton, Ohio 45404
39.781869,-84.158503

Genevieve's Ghost

When Sigmund Ksiezopolski built his store on Valley Street in the early 1900s, the family lived upstairs, and the store and deli were downstairs. His daughter Genevieve loved to play in the attic as a child and later worked in the store. She lived a long life and died at age 73. Many believe it is Genevieve's ghost who lingers in the building—her playful spirit plays pranks on guests visiting the restaurant there now, puffing out candles and moving glasses.

Bessie Little Bridge
AKA Ridge Avenue Bridge
Ridge Avenue
Dayton, Ohio 45405
39.782633, -84.20278

How Bessie Little Bridge Got Its Name

The Bessie Little Bridge—

There is a bridge on Ridge Avenue that crosses over the Stillwater River. Hikers on the Stillwater River Recreation Trail and travelers along the roadway have seen a young woman pacing about there before she disappears. The ghost belongs to Bessie Little, who boarded with Missus Dreese on South Jefferson Street in the city in the autumn of 1896. One September evening, she went for a ride with her boyfriend, Albert Frantz. Sometime after sunset, he shot her twice in the head and dumped her body into the Stillwater River.

Boys crossing the bridge found a tortoiseshell comb adorned with baubles and nearby, a trail of blood which they followed to the river. They found the corpse of the girl floating in the water. Her boyfriend was arrested for the crime, executed, and Bessie still walks the bridge

Dayton Masonic Center
525 W Riverview Avenue
Dayton, Ohio 45405
39.764676,-84.202824

Ghost in the Elevator

Visitors to the Masonic Center have been startled by spectral footsteps that appear to follow them around the building. Occasionally, the elevator is turned on by ghostly hands.

Victoria Theatre
138 N Main Street
Dayton, Ohio 45402
39.762334,-84.191837

The Ghost in the Curtains

It is not only floods and fires that have haunted this property, but ghosts walk the floors. One tale tells of an actor who went to her dressing room but did not appear in earthly form for the rest of her performance. She vanished and never returned until some began to see her as a ghost in a mirror. The scent of rose lingers in the air soon after.

Then, on January 3rd of 1904, 24-year-old John Alig, a stagehand for the theater, boozed it up for three straight days at Peter Schneider's saloon next to the Victoria. Finally, on January 5th, he downed carbolic acid and died a slow death by poisoning. After, those who came for the shows witnessed Alig's ghostly face peering through the front stage curtains before the start of the programs.

Old Courthouse
23 North Main
Dayton, Ohio 45402
39.759951,-84.191945

Mewlings of the Executed

The old courthouse and in the rear (to the left), where passersby hear eerie sounds. Image: Library of Congress.

In the mid to later 1800s, authorities used the property behind the old Dayton Courthouse at the corner of Third and Main streets for executions. Now, passersby occasionally pause as they hear mysterious mewling and cries from that area. When they seek out the cause, nothing is found.

Third Street
*444-598 W Third Street
Dayton, Ohio 45402
39.759618,-84.192868 to
39.758046,-84.20247*

Third Street Ghost

Third Street, where a ghost shows at the tail end of parades.

In 1824 and when Dayton was sparsely populated, John McAffee was about 21-years-old and a mopey young man who wandered into the city and met a local girl named Dorothy. Dorothy was pretty and sweet, and within a short amount of time, John married her, and the two settled down.

However, within just a few weeks, he began to notice that his new wife always seemed to be ill, bedridden, and prone to fits of seizures. Much of John's time and money was spent tending to the girl—giving her medicines and indulging her smallest needs. Looking after the needy Dorothy left him even moodier and finding solace in drinking heavily. It angered him that nobody told him she was so sickly before they married.

During this time, a woman in the neighborhood named Miss Hetty Shoop liked John, and the two began to have an affair. It was not long before Miss Hetty decided she wanted John to herself and persuaded him to kill his wife. One afternoon in June of 1824, when John went into Dorothy's room to give her medicine, he instead placed a 25 cent bottle of opium near her bedtable. "If you take this," he told Dorothy. "Your fits will be gone." And so she did as her husband bade her. Dorothy drank the poison; however, she did not die but lay there gasping for breath and making whimpers and cries. To finish her off, John jumped up on the bed, straddled the girl, and choked her to death. Then, realizing the horrible deed he had done, John quickly fled town.

The family discovered Dorothy murdered in her bed. For a long time, a posse searched out John McAffee, but his whereabouts remained unknown. The murdering man secreted himself in an isolated mining community. But he always longed, for reasons unknown, to come back to where he murdered his wife. And so when that need overwhelmed him, he returned to Dayton and the house where he killed poor Dorothy. The police caught him, and the courts sentenced the man to die.

It rained hard the days before John was executed. Still, thousands of the morbidly curious flocked to the makeshift scaffold located where Third Street nears the Miami River.

Those who traveled as far as twenty miles away waited with bated breath as the long procession marched along Third Street with John McAffee trudging along mopily at the end.

As the event began to unfold, a fog crept up from the river and into the muddy streets. The mist lingered around the scaffold and set a mood that seemed to excite the crowd. Finally, John was hanged, the pleased throngs dispersed, and life went on as usual in Dayton. But after that time, whenever there was a parade down Third Street following a few days of rain and a hard fog, those who happened to be around at the tail end of the procession would see John McAffee appear and trudge mopily along behind the last person until he vanished where he hanged.

Woodland Cemetery and Arboretum
Boy and Dog Road
Dayton, Ohio 45409
Grave: 39.742451, -84.177362

Johnny's Grave

Johnny's Grave at Woodland Cemetery and Arboretum showing the loyalty of a dog to a child even after death.

In 1860, five-year-old Johnny Morehouse lived with his mother, Mary Margaret, and father, John, in the rear of the family cobbler shop along the Miami and Erie Canal near what is now Patterson Boulevard in Dayton. On a blistering hot August day, Johnny was playing along the canal.

He fell into the dark depths, and his dog repeatedly tried to save him, but by the time he pulled the boy to the side of the canal, Johnny was dead.

After burying Johnny in Woodland Cemetery, his dog refused to leave his grave, staying by his young master even after death. Stories tell of visitors to the cemetery who saw the dog and left treats and food for him. The tradition continues. Trinkets are left on the grave to honor the loyal pup. The ghost of Johnny and his dog play at the cemetery, and the dog's playful bark blends with his tiny owner's giggles in the night.

Patterson Homestead
1815 Brown Street
Dayton, Ohio 45409
39.735219,-84.180969

Haunted House

Patterson Homestead —

There is a home on Brown Street in Dayton built by Revolutionary War veteran Robert Patterson, but eventually passing through family before being donated to the city as a museum. There is a haunting at the old home. One day, while volunteers were offering tours of the first floor of the house, the flight of steps was cordoned off so no visitors could enter the upstairs on their own.

As one guided tour passed beneath a room on the upper floor, the heavy sound of footsteps resounded above. Quickly, the leader broke from the group to herd whoever was upstairs back down. But when she got to the stairway and began to step on the first rung, she looked up to see a man in full military uniform. Then he vanished. They believed the ghost to be Robert Patterson.

Stivers School for the Arts
1313 E. Fifth Street
Dayton, Ohio 45402
39.75887,-84.175444

The Teacher's Restless Corpse

In the 1920s, a teacher was discovered dead in the indoor pool at Stivers School. She held a shattered pointer in one hand, and in her other, she clasped a mysterious locket. After she died, students began seeing her restless ghost floating above the old pool before she vanished. Even after the pool was covered with a floor and a classroom built overtop, a mysterious corpse-like mist formed where it once stood, and where the woman died.

Frankenstein's Castle
AKA Patterson Stone Tower
Hills and Dales MetroPark
Kettering, Ohio 45419
Parking at Paw Paw Camp:
39.710166, -84.179405
Short Walk to Tower:
39.709671, -84.180209

When Thunder Rolls

Patterson's Tower, also dubbed Frankenstein's Tower, for a lightning strike years ago.

Patterson's Tower was built in the early 1940s by boys with the National Youth Administration as an observation tower for the Community Country Club. They used stones salvaged from buildings the city had condemned. It was 50 steps to the building and 50 more to the lookout and offered a view 15 miles all around.

By the 1960s, the isolated area and the building became a place for teens to hang out and vandals to destroy the tower by tearing off shingles on the roofing and painting walls with graffiti. City recreational area guards placed a heavy iron gate with a lock around the tower, but trespassers constantly broke the lock and kicked out the bricks on the lookout tower to sneak inside.

On a stormy night in 1967, 17-year-old Ronnie Stevens and 16-year-old Peggy Harmeson slipped inside the building to escape the wrath of an oncoming storm. As the thunder crashed and the rain poured down, lightning hit the building killing Peggy, standing on the steps, and injuring Ronnie. Since then, on dark stormy nights when thunder rolls across the skies and lightning bursts from the clouds, a lone shadow wavers about the steps then staggers downward before vanishing.

Germantown Union Cemetery
11179 W Market Street
Germantown, Ohio 45327
39.623243,-84.388046

Dead Soldier Rising

During the Civil War, a young man from a Union-supporting family left home to support the Confederate cause. A Union soldier killed him in battle, but his father went south to retrieve his beloved son and buried him among his family at Germantown Union Cemetery. Occasionally, though, the ghost of the young soldier rises from the grave, and he searches about, confused at where he is, and looks for the comrades with whom he died.

Library Park
E Central Avenue
Miamisburg, Ohio 45342
39.641091, -84.284191

Library Park Phantom

In the late 1700s, Miamisburg added its first cemetery where the Civic Center stands today. However, as the town grew around the old lot and concerns over the safety of having corpses so close to underground drinking water systems, the graves were moved to a place farther outside town. For many years, this burial ground, called Village Cemetery, was used by the people in Miamisburg until, in the 1860s, Hillgrove Cemetery was founded.

The Village Cemetery eventually became Library Park. Families interred some of their dead to the new cemetery, but many stayed. Occasionally, those passing the grounds would note the phantom of a girl wearing cotton burial clothing floating across the overgrown lot and appearing deep in thought. Those who saw the spirit recognized it as a girl who was murdered years earlier. Then during the spring of 1884, the ghost began showing up nightly at 9:00 and crowds of the curious began turning out in huge numbers to ogle the girl gliding over the weeds and broken headstones with her hands behind her back and eyes to the ground.

Morgan County

**Brick Church Cemetery and
Historical Marker**
*1790 OH-376
Stockport, Ohio 43787
39.568537, -81.780252*

Dancing on the Grave

The grave of Captain Isaac Hook and a legend.

Captain Isaac Newton Hook is buried here next to the river with a unique grave. Captain Hook was a well-known businessman in Morgan County. He owned a general store in the mid-1840s and was also the captain of two steamboats on the Muskingum River. Folks always talked that he did not get along with his second wife. When he passed on, he had an unusual tomb made with a rounded roof, 'so his wife could not dance on top of his grave when he died.'

McConnelsville Courthouse
15 E Main Street
McConnelsville, Ohio 43756
39.648768,-81.852973
Morgan County Historical
Society

Bad Luck Revolver

McConnelsville Courthouse—

In September of 1905, a person with schizophrenia named Wood Stuard ambushed and shot McConnelsville City Marshal Horace Porter in an alleyway. Stuard was under the delusion that the marshal was trying to hunt him down. A judge found him unfit for trial and sent him to an asylum. After, Stuard's gun fell into the hands of Francis Parsons, a young attorney who placed it in his office safe.

Years later, Francis Parsons prosecuted the case of Missus Francis Allen in McConnelsville for murdering her baby. John Smith, who found the baby's grave on his property, suffered a heart attack. Doctor Lucius Culver, the main witness to the murder, became paralyzed during the trial and could not speak, and soon after, died. Finally, Francis Parsons committed suicide—with the gun he pulled from the safe that killed the marshal.

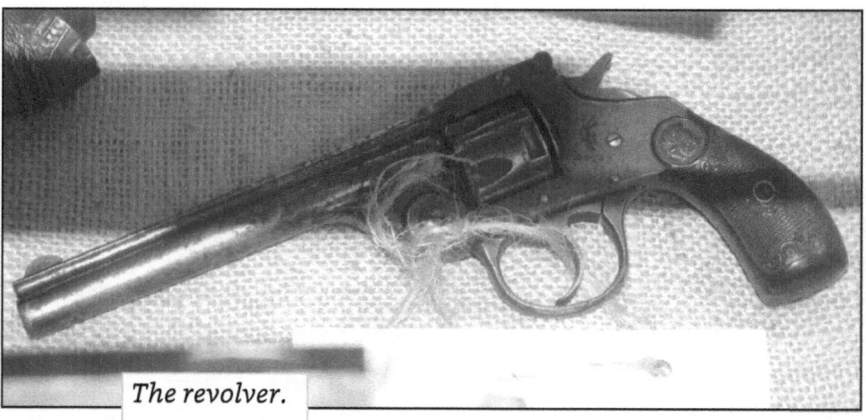

The revolver.

Francis Parsons haunts the courthouse. Some walking in the hallways have heard his footsteps passing by. You can view the bad luck revolver at the Morgan County Historical Society—142 East Main Street, McConnelsville.

Twin City Opera House
15 West Main Street
McConnelsville, Ohio 43756
39.648985,-81.853493

The Specter Usher

The Twin City Opera House opened in 1892 and has been used for many things including vaudeville acts, high school commencements, and movies. Ushers were used to collect tickets and to seat the guests. One of the ushers who was well-liked by those visiting the opera house was Everett Miller. After death, his ghost returned to walk the aisles.

Muskingum County

Stumpy Hollow
10245 Norwich Drive
Norwich, Ohio 43767
39.982859, -81.796340

Stumpy

Stumpy Hollow—

In the early 1800s, the Federal Government built the National Road connecting the eastern and western states. In Ohio, along the route were the larger towns of Cambridge and Zanesville, and about halfway between the two was the smaller village of Norwich—each providing stagecoach stops along the road. It is near Norwich, where downhill winding curves made for more than a few harrowing experiences for stagecoach drivers.

One particularly terrifying encounter was on August 20th, 1835. Thirty-five-year-old Christopher Baldwin, who was a librarian of the American Antiquarian Society, was traveling by stagecoach to research ancient burial mounds around southern Ohio. As the stagecoach driver sped through the turns, a farmer with a drove of hogs swept out into the street. The pigs spooked the horses, the stage overturned, and Baldwin died.

A few years would pass after the incident, and during the 1840s, the village doctor was visiting a sick patient around midnight. His travels took him down the main street of Norwich, just past the cemetery, and then along a path that leads through a dark hollow. It was here that he heard rustling sounds in the brush along one bank and credited it to deer moving in to rest for the night. He had made these nightly treks often, and the town was safe—he felt no fear. That is until something strange barreled upward from the far end of the hollow, rushing straight at him at a fast pace.

The doctor towed back on the reins. His horse stumbled backward, but not before the man's eyes took in the terrifying sight. It was a ghostly figure atop a horse—and it had no head—just a stumpy knob at the end of his neck! He could not believe what he saw. As his wide eyes blinked, the horse and rider completely disappeared. Then the doctor's horse reared, almost tossing him from his saddle before bolting back toward town.

The doctor told his story to neighbors and they laughed, one even deciding to disprove him. At midnight, he went into the hollow on foot. He, too, found himself face to face with the headless rider. This ghostly figure would show in many forms, some even describing it as a man-faced dog.

But all knew whose ghost it was—nicknamed Stumpy for the stubby knob of the headless neck. It was that of Christopher Baldwin—a spirit stuck on earth and never able to get to his destination to finish his work and who rode from his place of death to the cemetery where he was buried.

Prospect Place
12150 Main Street
Trinway, Ohio 43842
40.134857, -82.012063

The Remorseful Phantom

Prospect Place—

In the 1800s, George Adams built a mansion near Trinway. It had many rooms, inside plumbing, and special rooms in the basement to harbor slaves while escaping to the north. He was married twice and had ten children who grew up happily in the home there.

The family—

Among his children was the eldest daughter named Anna. When Anna became of marriageable age, she wed wealthy William Cox. The two lived happily together for years, and her father passed the house on to Anna. The couple, after, had extravagant balls and parties, living a life of luxury. However, as the money began to run out, William left for a business trip and never returned. Years passed, then those in the home often talked of seeing the ghostly form of William ambling around the rooms and halls. Most believed he was looking for Anna out of remorse for leaving.

William— Anna—

More legends and hauntings in the home.

The Bounty Hunter—George Adams operated a mill on the Ohio and Erie Canal. When his company took flour to New Orleans, the boats would return with escaping slaves. One night, a bounty hunter bribed a farmer and found out that the Adams had fleeing slaves hidden in their home. Those in the household turned the bounty hunter away and watched him walk off into the night. He was found hanging in the barn's loft on the property, and field workers buried him in an unmarked grave far from the house. After, a dark phantom-like figure began showing up and strolling around the old barn before disappearing within.

Girl on the Balcony—A housemaid working in the home had taken ill. The family gave her a room and prepared a bed for the girl. But, during the night, her fever raged high and senseless, she walked off the front balcony. Visitors to the mansion have seen her floating in the air high above the front porch where the old patio once stood.

Escaped Slave—A slave died of sickness in the cellar rooms. In years past, some have seen her wandering the rooms there.

Constance Cox—Constance was the 21-year-old adopted daughter of Anna Adams-Cox. After she died of lung fever in September of 1898, some heard ghostly gasps in her room.

Train Wreck Victims—After a train wreck in December of 1912, the home was allegedly opened as a storage area for the bodies of at least eleven dead, some of them children, until they could be picked up by family. Occasionally, the sounds of ghostly children playing are heard within the old home.

Saint Matthews Episcopal Cemetery (Old Stone Church)
Stone Church Road
Adamsville, Ohio 43802
40.127802,-81.916019

The Caretaker

The St Matthews Episcopal Church was once on Old Stone Church Road. Only its cemetery remains. Many years ago, the old caretaker who once tended to the church and grounds died suddenly. After the grass began to grow up around the old graves, the headstones started to topple, and the church burned down.

It was around this time that people passing the cemetery would see a man in coveralls, work boots, and knit hat walk down the steps from the cemetery to the road. If they stopped their cars, he would approach them before vanishing. Those who shine a flashlight at the old, dead caretaker can see it shine through him.

Pickaway County

Stages Pond State Nature Preserve
4890 Hagerty Road
Ashville, Ohio 43103
39.671537,-82.936705

Pond of the Dead Mules

A wagon and team of mules lay at the bottom of Stage's Pond outside Ashville. A story about their haunting the pond area has been passed down from a local family to volunteers and staff at the preserve and verified by a descendant of the farmer.

Sometimes when a good storm rolls over Stages Pond State Nature Preserve, you can hear the deep thud of hooves bolting across muddy roads and then, the splash of swampy water as if something huge is bursting headlong into the boggy marsh there. Afterward, terrified screams echo ghostly cries in the air before they vanish as if swallowed up.

More than one visitor to the preserve has been startled by this commotion. When they ask locals, they do not always believe the truth told—that on a muggy August day in the 1800s, a farmer who lived across Ward Road was taking in the hay. A storm blew across the fields, and he ran to get out of the rain. Lightning bolted across the sky along with an explosion of thunder right after. The wagon team he was using to take in the hay bolted down over the road and across the muddy land around Stage's Pond. Straight into the marshy, quick-sand-like muck they went, mired and fighting until they sank so deeply they could not be retrieved. And now, only their ghostly echoes fill the thick air on hot summer nights, and right before a storm when lightning fills the sky and thunder rolls nearby.

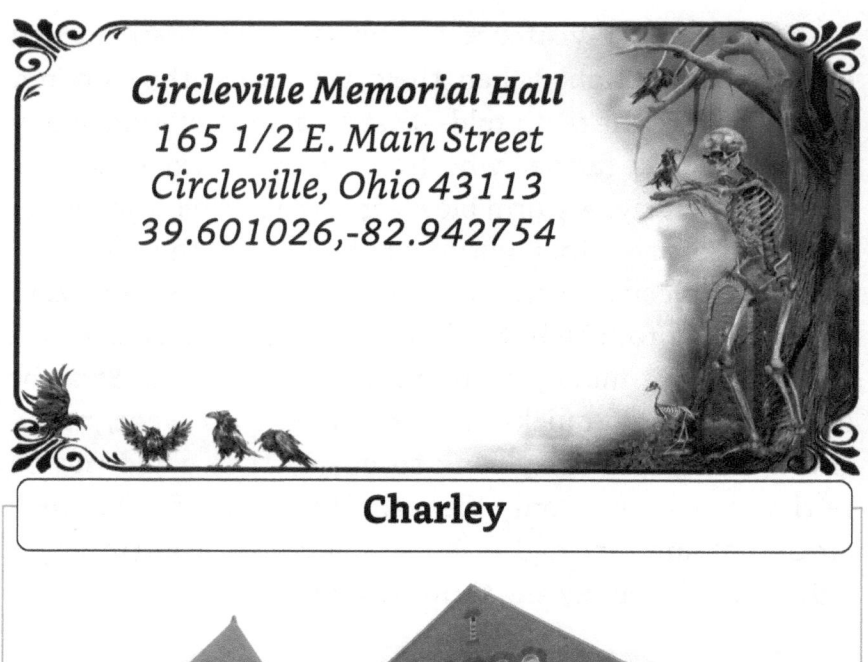

Circleville Memorial Hall
165 1/2 E. Main Street
Circleville, Ohio 43113
39.601026,-82.942754

Charley

The sound of ghostly footsteps pacing in the upper floors is believed to be those from a young man named Charley, whose headstone was mysteriously left in the cellar.

Pike County

Evergreen Union Cemetery
State Route 220
Waverly, Ohio 45690
39.11720, -82.98390

Mourning Mary

Local legend says the statue of Mary Emmitt once held a gun in the clasp of the right hand. Mary had committed suicide. Now her ghost walks the cemetery, mourning her death.

Pike Lake State Park
Pike Lake Road
Bainbridge, Ohio 45612
39.159920, -83.218545

Haunted Stump

WILDCAT HOLLOW NATURE TRAIL
1.2 MILE ONE-WAY

Pike Lake State Park—

Back in the olden days, when someone needed to clear land for a house or a field, all the neighbors for miles around would come together and help out. They would cut the trees down to stumps, chop them into logs, and with handspikes, roll them into a pile, and have a bonfire. It was called a 'log rolling,' and it was a time of picnics and festivities for the whole community. All the while, they took turns tending the fires. Once in a while, a spark would fly, or a flame would lick the hem of a shirt or dress.

At one particular log burning in the 1860s where Pike Lake State Park is now, a young woman of about 18 years of age was working with the others poking and prodding the limbs and branches to keep the fire strong and the wood burning, easing her way around one fire when a huge, flaming log broke loose from the top of the pile and careened downward. As she had her stick in her hand, the log rolled on it so the young woman keeled inward, and she could not release her fingers. She fell forward and was dragged to the earth until her palms slapped hard on the ground. The log rolled right over her hands and to her wrists.

Help came quickly, but not fast enough. The girl's hands were so severely burned, as she was wringing them, they fell right off and on to a stump. She died, and for years after, those passing the stump would see two charred ghost hands rising from the stump or feel their hot grasp on their ankles as they passed by.

Old Hermit Trail
1444-1686 US-23
Waverly, Ohio 45690
39.198735, -82.978547
(Private Property)

The Mislaid Bones

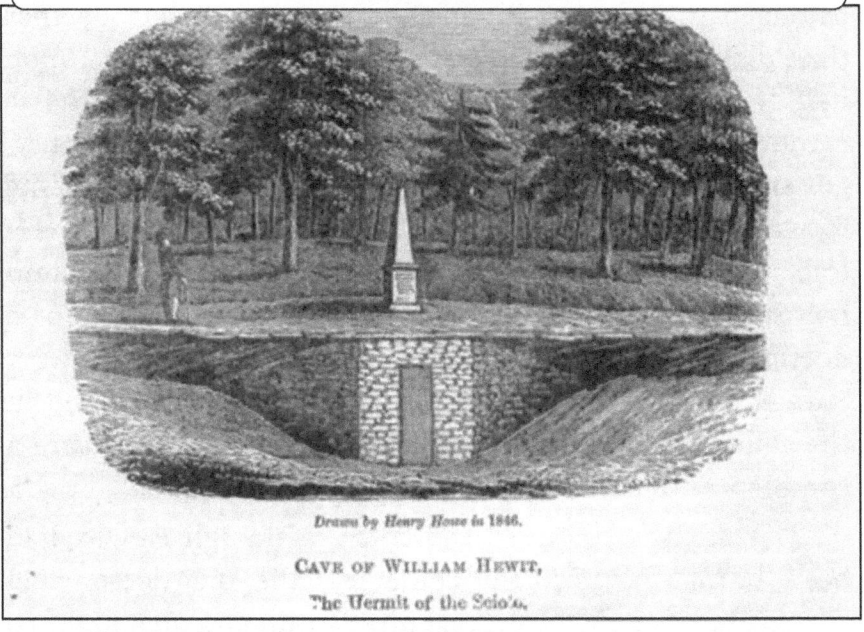

Drawn by Henry Howe in 1846.

CAVE OF WILLIAM HEWITT,

The Hermit of the Scioto.

In the early years of Ohio, a hermit lived in a cave along what is now State Route 23 and George Hollow Road. His name was William Hewitt, and he was a huge, hulking man often seen walking about in buckskin leather leggings, a cap, hunting shirt, and moccasins. Few came close to the old hermit as he rarely bathed or washed his knotted hair. When he was around 70-years-old, he became ill. Doctor William Blackstone tended to Hewitt until the hermit died.

After he died, the old recluse would have been forgotten except that his ghost began to show up trudging along the old road by his cave home on half-moon nights just after a rain. He frightened passersby when they stopped to see if he needed help, and he vanished into the air. As everyone knows, ghosts only show up when they have not completed some task, or some wrongdoing must be righted. There were all sorts of speculations about why Hewitt returned—the betrayal of a woman in his youth or treachery of a brother over the family estate after his father's death.

Then many years later in 1852, a stonemason named Edward Vester was digging a cellar of the home that once belonged to Doctor William Blackstone, who had by that time died. Four feet deep and near one wall, he came upon half of a skeletal frame of a man. Within a few days and as rumors began to course their way through the community, a nephew of the doctor who lived in Circleville came forward with a second partial skeletal frame of a man. He told authorities that before his uncle died, he had given him half of a man's bones because he too was studying to be a doctor. They had belonged to the hermit William Hewitt. Sure enough, when they put half of the skeleton found in the cellar with the bones the nephew offered, they were a complete set belonging to the large old hermit.

The nephew divulged the truth. Although Hewitt had been buried in Waverly Cemetery, the old doctor had returned to the graveyard just after a rain and on a night so dark that the half-moon light barely allowed the trees to cast shadows on the ground. The earth was soft from the rain, and he easily dug up the remains of William Hewitt. Doctor Blackstone dissected the corpse, boiled away the rotting flesh, and hung part of the skeleton in his office until this grisly trophy was given to his nephew much later. He had secretly buried the remaining bones in his garden.

Nobody would have ever known about the doctor's ghastly deed and why the old hermit returned in ghostly form had his old home not been expanded to include the garden where the stonemason discovered the bones. After the unearthing, the spectral form of William Hewitt no longer frightened travelers along the road that was later expanded and became State Route 23.

Cave in 1910.

Hewitt's Cave, near Chillicothe, Ohio.

In the 1840s after the hermit's death, the president of the road erected a monument over the cave stating: "Wm. Hewitt, the Hermit, occupied this cave fourteen years, while all was a wilderness around him. He died in 1834 aged 70 years." In the 1950s, the road was made a four-laner and the monument was moved to Scioto Trail State Park.

From Ohio State 1915 Archeological Atlas, Ohio Published by Fred J. Heer in 1912 showing the cave.

Preble County

Old Haunted House in Somerville
Somerville, Ohio 45064

Old Haunted House

Where a ghost once chased two farmers—

In February of 1910, a rabid dog was running freely in Somerville. Local farmers grabbed up their guns to kill the mutt and spare other animals from getting the disease. During the day, nobody was able to find the dog, and most believed it had headed out of the county or went off to die. By dusk, most had headed for home. However, word came out that some men had noticed from afar while tracking the dog that lights were on at an abandoned home.

Farmers Dan Thomas and Andy Neanover took it upon themselves to investigate, snatched up their shotguns, and walked through the snow to the house. When they came to the broken front door, something nearly 8 feet tall, lean and pink, burst from within and through the door past them. Then it vanished. Shaken, the men left for home, and within a few moments, both felt the strange sensation that something was following them. Sure enough, behind the two, there was a mysterious shadowy figure lurking.

The two bolted for Thomas's house, finally reaching the yard surrounded by a tall wooden enclosure. Thomas and Neanover abandoned making their way to the gate on the far side and instead began to climb over the fence. Before they could fully scale the boards to make it into the safety of the yard, the spook took hold of both men's legs until they kicked loose, ran to the house, and closed the door behind them.

Over the years, many people witnessed the ghostly happenings at the home—strange groans and whimpers and the creaking of ghostly feet to wooden floors. Eventually, the house fell to ruins. But few still traveled near after dark for fear of the phantom—an old man named Jake Beatty, who had hanged himself within nearly 35 years earlier.

Richland County

Bissman Building
193 N. Main Street
Mansfield, Ohio 44902
40.763756, -82.515534

The Head by the Elevator

The Bissman Building—

The Bissman Company was a wholesale receiver and distributor of grocery goods for Mansfield, including coffee, cigars, and alcoholic beverages from 1886 to the 2000s. Those within the building have seen a decapitated head lying next to an old elevator before it fades away entirely.

It supposedly belongs to F.W. Simon whose last day of work was in 1911. As he left the upper building floor and climbed into the elevator, he whipped his head out quickly to give the last goodbye to his coworkers. His head caught between the doors as the elevator began to move, slicing it from his body.

Mansfield Women's Club
145 Park Avenue West
Mansfield, Ohio 44902
40.758597, -82.521026

Lucretia

Mansfield Women's Club—

An old home on Park Avenue belonged to Henry and Lucretia Hedges and was later bequeathed to the Mansfield Women's Club. Lucretia's ghost visits once in a while as guests have seen her shadowy figure flitting about, followed by a chilly waft of air.

Renaissance Performing Arts Theatre
Former Ohio Theatre
138 Park Avenue West
Mansfield, Ohio 44902
40.759277, -82.520522

Murder at the Ohio Theatre

Renaissance Performing Arts Theatre, former Ohio Theatre—

The specter of a man makes a tottering pace back and forth, back and forth in a room at the Renaissance Theatre. Another darker entity skulks around the lobby, bent and sauntering deliberately slow as if keeping a devious and wary eye of his surroundings. The ghosts are explained like this—In October of 1929, a gunman wearing a suit with the collar turned up and a black mask entered the Ohio Theatre.

He walked into the office of Edward Rafter during the showing of 'The Green Murder Case,' thrust out a hand with a gunny sack, and demanded the theatre manager fill the bag with money from the safe.

Rafter turned and pretended to open the safe, then out of fear, suddenly whipped around and lunged at the thief. After a hand-to-hand struggle, gunshots rang out, and Rafter received a bullet to his head. He died three days later from the wound. The would-be thief ran away without a cent from the safe.

The police never found the murderer, but they found a bloodstained gunnysack that was meant to hold the loot and a black mask. So now Rafter paces his office, forever holding on to those moments before his death. And the dark man who murdered Rafter eventually showed up in phantom form, too, perhaps dying in another botched robbery. His return is most likely to seek out the money from the safe he could never steal.

Ohio State Reformatory
100 Reformatory Road
Mansfield, Ohio 44905
40.784327, -82.502306

The Reformatory

Ohio State Reformatory—

During the time the Ohio State Reformatory in Mansfield was open, 1896 to 1990, over 154,000 inmates passed through the gates. The prison took in offenders who were too old for juvenile corrections, or who also committed less severe crimes than those sent to prison at the Ohio State Penitentiary in Columbus. The goal of this institution was to reform inmates with education, religion, and learning a trade.

Not everyone made it out of the reformatory. Two-hundred people died at the jail including guards killed in escape attempts. Frank Hanger, a 48-year-old guard, was beaten to death with an iron bar by Chester Probaski and Elza Chandler in October of 1932. He was making rounds in the disciplinary block, and Chandler was crouching near a cupboard. Chandler was on an extended stay in solitary confinement. Prison wardens shuffled both murderers to the electric chair.

The family of the warden lived at the reformatory. In November of 1950, the warden's wife, Helen Bauer Glattke, died of pneumonia several days after an accidental discharge of a gun in the superintendent's home inside the prison. While reaching into a closet to retrieve a jewelry box, the gun discharged, injuring the woman. Arthur Lewis Glattke, her husband, died following a heart attack suffered in his office on February 10th, 1959. This is the closet where the gun discharged, injuring Helen, which eventually caused her death. Her ghostly voice is heard quietly chattering in the room and around the closet.

The Mansfield Reformatory Preservation Society runs the remaining parts of the building—the original East (and six tiers of the largest free-standing steel cell block in the world) and West Cell Blocks and administration section. The building is open for tours. If you go, expect to see, hear, or feel ghosts. We did. My 4-year-old shushed me with forefinger to lips because, as he put it: "Mommy, there's a man trying to sleep in that bed." And I took a picture of my daughter with a full-body apparition showing up in the image.

A ghost walks into the room behind her.

A priceless family picture—my daughter digesting that her brother is telling her there is a ghost a foot away. And he is not a happy ghost. We woke him up. Shhhh.

*Mt Olive Cemetery
4945 Opossum Run or Tucker
Bellville, Ohio 44813
40.638520, -82.443223*

Bloody Mary

The tree, center, right after it was burned by vandals and before it was cut down by criminals later.

There is a cemetery secreted on the grounds of a camp outside Mansfield. In this graveyard, there was laid a lonely stone with the name Mary Jane engraved upon it. Above the grave, a massive tree once stood tall and mighty before vandals snatched up a chainsaw, placed the blade against the trunk, and cut it to the ground. But since the 1960s and before it fell, teens from the nearby communities would come to the grave and stand above it. They would stare at the aged tree and lone grave below because legends had been passed on to them that the woman entombed beneath it was a witch. After family buried her, a cross appeared on the tree's bark, and the sap flowed blood-red down its trunk.

Those who visited the grave would chant softly, "Bloody Mary" and wait for her to rise. Those who jumped over her grave and spit on it would come to some horrible death.

We are not the first to make nighttime pilgrimages with ghoulish intent to sites that sate some morbid fascination with death and the supernatural. In the 1800s, interest in the supernatural became quite a trend with seances, Ouija boards, fortune-telling, and scary parlor games. One popular game for young women was gathering in the dark and performing a ritual where each took turns walking a flight of steps backward, holding a candle in one hand and a mirror in the other. As they progressed upward, each stared into the mirror, and if a man's face appeared, it would be that of the husband she would marry. But if the skull of the grim reaper appeared, she would die before she wed.

As years passed, this game transformed into a girl standing in front of a mirror in a dimly lit bathroom with the door shut chanting with her eyes closed. Some would repeat, "I believe in Mary Worth," while others chanted, "I believe in Bloody Mary," or even "I believe in Mary Wails." It was usually 13 times. The girl would open her eyes and stare into the mirror, waiting for a witch to appear covered in blood screaming curses through the glass reflection. There are countless variations of the identity of Bloody Mary, from a local murder victim to a witch and even the 5-year reign in the 1500s of fervently Catholic Mary I. She seized the English throne and burned 280 Protestants at the stake as heretics. She was nicknamed Bloody Mary.

In Mansfield, where the Bloody Mary of local lore started, many will be compelled to take a trek to Mt Olive Cemetery. The headstone is gone, the tree dragged away. But nighttime still comes to the cemetery, and some will return to chant her name at the place Mary Jane still lays. And maybe her story will be passed along as all folklore should be.

Malabar Farm State Park
4050 Bromfield Road
Lucas, Ohio 44843
40.650086, -82.395078

Ghost of Celia Rose

Celia Rose—The sweet face of a killer— or not.

It is difficult to imagine this cute little farmhouse complete with picket fence was the location for a disturbing triple murder concocted with deceit, rat poison, and cottage cheese.

It was a warm June 24 morning in the summer of 1896. David Rose, a local miller who lived in the community of Pleasant Valley, made a mad rush for the nearby doctor in Newville. His wife, Rebecca, had become violently sick two hours after breakfast with vomiting and convulsions. Before David returned to the house with the village doctor, he would also succumb to the same mysterious sickness.

It would not be long after that David's 39-year-old son, Walter, was found along the road overcome with the same symptoms.

Six days later, on June 30th, David Rose died an agonizing death. On July 4th, Walter would die. For a short time, Rebecca seemed to be recuperating. She appeared in good health, only to give way to the condition a little less than a month from the day she got sick. She, too, died. The youngest member of the family, a mentally disabled daughter named Celia, fondly called Ceely, was the only one who would not become ill from the symptoms. Autopsies later revealed poisoning with arsenic rat poison—Rough on Rats was what caused the deaths.

Fingers pointed to the childlike Celia Rose. Although she had attended school, she was much farther behind than the other children and spent most of her time alone. Celia did, at times, find it difficult to differentiate between right and wrong, and her stuttering left her the object of ridicule by other children.

To make matters worse, the young Celia who most thought odd for her disability, was infatuated with a neighbor boy who did not return her fondness, mistaking his kindness for affection. Her innocent trips to visit him had become so frequent, the young man's father had spoken to David Rose, asking him to curtail Celia's visits and affections. Her father, a kind man who was said to rarely scold his daughter, reprimanded her. Some believed this set the circumstances leading to the family's deaths. During her family's illness and after their deaths, she seemed blissfully unaware of the weight of the situation, and she probably had no clue what she had done would make them go away forever.

A local prosecutor connived with Theresa Davis, a former classmate of Celia, to trick her into confessing. Theresa pretended to be Celia's friend which must have been elating for the young woman who had never had a chum before. Theresa told Celia she had kept the secrets of others who had done things to those who had been mean to them, and Celia could confide anything to her. Celia allegedly confessed she had poisoned her family with arsenic and that she had added it to their morning cottage cheese because her father disapproved of her seeing the boy next door.

Twenty-three-year-old Celia Rose was found guilty of the murders. The verdict took only an hour. She was sentenced to life in prison, then acquitted on the grounds of insanity. She was sent to the Lima State Hospital and died there on March 14, 1934. The little white farmhouse of Celia Rose and her family is at Malabar Farm State Park. It is haunted. Celia's ghostly younger self returns to the home and peers through the windows.

Watch for Celia peering through the windows when you pass by. Did she poison her family or not? Some say Celia was manipulated into making a confession, and that is why her ghost returns—to right the wrong of those who coerced this young woman to lie for the real killer because she had no one left in the world to defend her.

Scioto County

Old McDaniel Hermit Place
225—288 Ghost Hollow Road
Lucasville, Ohio 45648
38.86631,-83.029229

Ghost Hollow

Ghost Hollow Road not far from Portsmouth. The hollow is on private property.

In a rural area between Lucasville and Portsmouth, there is a dark dell called Ghost Hollow with a road leading past it by the same name. Very few nowadays know how the isolated hollow got its name. The story goes like this—Old Man McDaniel lived alone in a large home in a deep hollow.

He kept to himself, very rarely speaking to neighbors or leaving his house. He died, most say, by shooting himself in the head, but because of his reclusive nature, it was a long time before anyone discovered his remains not far from the front door of his house. By the time neighbors realized the old man had not left his property in many days, they knocked on his door to check on him. When he did not answer, they entered the home and found insects and vermin had eaten what remained of his head. All that was left was his rotting corpse from the neck down.

After, the home got a reputation for being haunted. Travelers passing by saw a headless man at the door of the house, and anyone who had been a tenant of the home left in only a few days of renting as they were awakened around midnight by ghastly groans and moans.

In December of 1896, Frank Crowe, a prominent farmer near Lucasville who lived near the hollow, his son James, and a Miss Clara McCorkle were heading homeward after a get-together at the home of Frank's brother. It was late in the evening, so Frank agreed to chaperone his son and the girl. To save time, they took a shortcut down a hillside that dropped into a certain dark patch of a hollow where Old Man McDaniel's abandoned house sat alone in a pocket of woods. As they came upon the house, something moved near the dilapidated porch. As the four gazed at the home in the full moonlight, the specter of a headless man came through the open front door of the old house, paused momentarily just outside, then began to walk toward them on the overgrown lawn with arms flailing about. The three were so startled that they fled the scene. For many years after, carriages of people would come from surrounding communities to drive past the haunted house on the lane they dubbed Ghost Hollow Road to get a glimpse of the headless specter lurching toward them with arms thrashing around.

Otway School
6864 Ohio 73
Otway, Ohio 45657
38.866331,-83.189373

The Guard

Otway School—

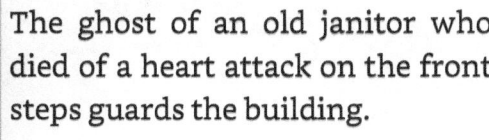
A ghostly boy watching out the window of the left door.

The ghost of an old janitor who died of a heart attack on the front steps guards the building.

Vinton County

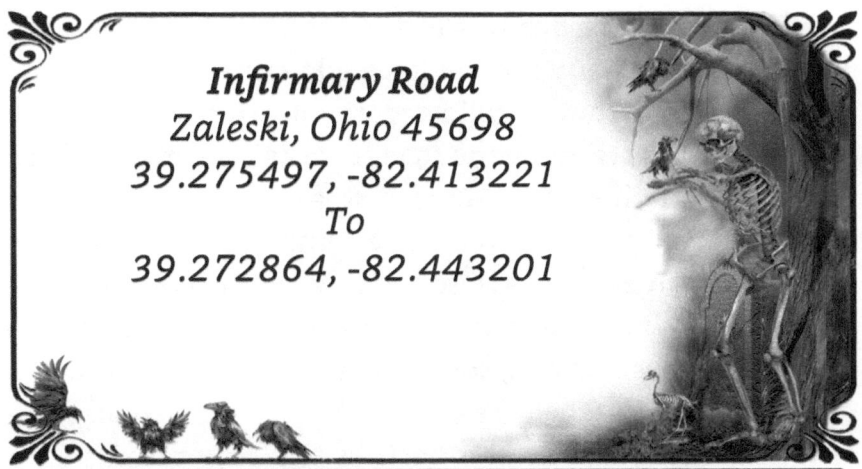

Infirmary Road
Zaleski, Ohio 45698
39.275497, -82.413221
To
39.272864, -82.443201

White Thing of Infirmary Road

Shry Hill on Infirmary Road where a man took a wild, ghostly ride.

Outside of Zaleski, an old gravel road weaves its way to the bustling town of McArthur. At one time, the Vinton County Infirmary and its little cemetery were settled on the path, and such those in the community called it Infirmary Road. Little farmsteads were spread far apart along its route, and between fields and meadows, there were long patches of deep, dark forest.

Most people avoided this little stretch of road after dusk. It had a ghost. Many reputable people talked about it long ago and retold that it followed them after dark. Alonzo Eckelberry was traveling the road from Zaleski on horseback one night in the late 1800s. Just as he passed the old Herrold's Mill along Racoon Creek and was in sight of a small homestead, he saw something white keeping pace beside him. When the man hastened his horse with a gentle tickle of his heels to ribs, the white thing sped up. When he slowed, it also matched the pace. As he passed the house, the specter jumped up on the back of the frightened man's horse.

Startled, Eckelberry turned his horse around to speed back to Zaleski. Looking backward, he could see the ghost perched atop the rear of his ride, but the horse appeared unaware. Then, when he got to a slope called Shry Hill for the family living at the peak, the ghost jumped off. Eckelberry lost no time in widening the expanse between himself and the horrifying apparition. And he refused, like many, to travel that route after dusk again.

Warren County

Old McClung Home
101 E Main Street
Mason, Ohio 45040
39.360199,-84.308943

A Murder in Mason

Old McClung Home—

In 1901, a wealthy and reclusive old man and woman were living in a cozy red brick house on a corner of Main Street in the small farming community of Mason. Neighbors rarely spoke to the two, and most of the time, Rebecca did not go outside and instead was often seen peering out the windows. One morning, the old man named John McClung went out to feed his horse. Upon returning less than an hour later, he found his wife Rebecca dead on the floor in a pool of blood with her head beaten. A bloody piece of ash stove wood lay nearby.

When he awakened a neighbor and the police arrived, there was blood on John's clothing. When asked if he had murdered his wife, John stated, "I might have done it, and I might not. If I did, I don't remember anything of it." Police arrested the man and charged him with murder. However, during the trial, it was never concluded if someone had broken into the home to steal money or if John had killed his wife in a fit of anger. John McClung was found not guilty in court and died a few years later. The building, over time, has changed hands. And it is haunted. Rebecca's ghost still peers out the windows.

Kings Island—Dog Street Cemetery
Kings Island Drive
Maineville, Ohio 45039
39.350226,-84.267793

Missouri Jane

Dog Street Cemetery by the parking lot at Kings Island is well over 200 years old. Most settlers buried here lived to a ripe old age of 60 or 70. But some like Missouri Jane Galeenor died at a young age. Some believe Missouri is the little ghost girl wandering the cemetery and inside the amusement park. Kings Island opened in 1972, but for well over a half-century, people have reported the ghostly apparition of a child in a blue dress working her way among the graves and have seen her while riding the park's train.

Old Peters Cartridge Factory
1915 Grandin Road
Kings Mills, Ohio 45034
39.351448,-84.241578

The Old Powder Mill

The old cartridge factory at Kings Mill—

In Kings Mills, the Loveland Bike Trail runs past an old set of brick buildings tucked into a wooded hollow along the Little Miami River. Those riding the route have been startled by distorted and bent forms crossing their path. Others have seen ghostly faces peering from windows and hear a baby's shrill cry before it stops abruptly. There once was a powder mill here built by J.W. King and his nephew where shotgun shells and rifle cartridges were made.

Then, in July of 1890, a train car collided with two load cars filled with 800 kegs of gunpowder along the Little Miami Railroad. In a chain reaction, 800 more barrels exploded. Twelve people died. One of them was a baby.

The Golden Lamb Inn/ Restaurant
27 S Broadway Street
Lebanon, Ohio 45036
39.43384,-84.208817

Ghosts at the Golden Lamb

The Golden Lamb—

In 1871, lawyer Clement Vallandingham was 51-years-old when he fatally shot himself attempting to reenact a shooting for display in a court trial occurring in Lebanon. He was in a second-floor room of the Golden Lamb, and since his death, guests have seen his ghost hovering around the hallway and room.

But Vallandingham is not the only resident ghost at the inn. Eliza Clay, daughter of politician Henry Clay and his wife, Lucretia, passed away at the inn in 1825. Henry Clay was John Quincy Adams's Secretary of State during those days. While traveling by stagecoach with his family to Washington in August of that year, the family interrupted their trip in Lebanon. Their 12-year-old daughter had taken ill with typhoid. They found a place to stay at the Golden Lamb (then called the Ferguson House), but after nearly a month of the illness, the girl died on August 11, 1825. Travelers staying at the inn have long seen Eliza's ghost within the building.

Sources:

-Allen County:
Celia Rose—www.findagrave.com/cgi-bin/fg.cgi?page=cr&CRid=43582
Ironwood News Record September 19, 1896
Daily Iowa Capital August 14, 1896
Decatur Evening Bulletin August 14, 1896
Galveston Daily News August 14, 1896
Newark Daily Advocate October 21, 1896
Portsmouth Daily Times October 14, 1896
Reno Weekly Gazette And Stockman August 20, 1896
Triple Murder: The Crimes Committed by Celia Rose By Brett Mitchell
Fort Amanda:
Fort Amanda State Park Monument Info:John Stanton
Annabelle Davis:
Grave Addiction: www.graveaddiction.com/ridgeway.html
-Harrison, R. H. (1880). *Atlas of Allen County, Ohio from Records and Original Surveys*. Philadelphia: R.H. Harrison.
-http://www.usgennet.org/usa/topic/colonial/census/1840/1840oh_a.html
Bloody Bridge:
© Can Stock Photo Inc. / Hofmeester
The Bloody Bridge- Old Papers Recall Bloody Tragedy in the Palmy Days of the Canal. May 15th, 1908 Delphos Daily Herald Newspaper
-Butler:
Train Wrecks
GenDisasters—Events That Touched Our Ancestors' Lives
http://uglybridges.com/1397449—MAUDS HUGHES RD over NORFOLK & SOUTHERN RR Butler County, Ohio.
-Champaign County:
Library of Congress. Johnston, Frances Benjamin, 1864-1952, photographer
-Clark County:
Black Cemetery
http://www.rootsweb.ancestry.com/~ohclark/cemetery/blackcemetery.htm
http://www.findagrave.com/cgi-bin/fg.cgi?page=cr&CRid=39924&CScnty=2051&
Hertzler: http://www.findagrave.com/cgi-bin/fg.cgi?page=gr&GSln=hertzler&GSiman=1&GScid=40837&GRid=44773663&
National Register of Historic Places Clark County
Wilmington College—A History of Wilmington College—Dr. O.F. Boyd
Doan's Horse—Kilikilik - Heidelberg College Student Newspaper
http://www.heidelberg.edu/sites/default/files/admin/images/Kil_119_04.pdf
Ethyl Hanley-Haunted Places: The National Directory : Ghostly Abodes, Sacred Sites, Ufo By Dennis William Hauck
Honeymoon Ghost—Disturbed Honeymoon-Hutchinson Daily News, 3/5/1903.
https://www.findagrave.com/memorial/82311966/emma-c.-heydinger
Brownella Cottage -
Ohiohauntedplaces.com—ohiohauntedplaces.com/?cat=9
Galion Historical Society -www.galionhistory.com
National Register of Historic Places listings in Crawford County, Ohio
-Cuyahoga
http://cleveland.about.com/od/clevelandhistory/ss/hauntedclev_2.htm
National Register Information System". National Register of Historic Places. National Park Service. 2009-03-13.
Armory image: Courtesy Columbus Metropolitan Library
-Cuyahoga County
Lake View Cemetery:
http://www.deadohio.com/lakeview1.**htm**
http://www.findagrave.com/cgi-bin/fg.cgi?page=cr&CRid=41762
Agora:
Encyclopedia of Cleveland History: Agora Ballroom
http://www.clevelandagora.com/History
Erie Street Cemetery:
Case Western Reserve University
Erie Street Cemetery By John D. Cimperman
Franklin Castle
The Times Recorder: Jan 19, 1975 - Zanesville, Ohio
Tiedemann House (Franklin Castle) by: Jim Dubelko—
http://clevelandhistorical.org/items/show/531#.UgBTVLbD_cs

www.hauntedamericatours.com: http://www.hauntedamericatours.com/
hauntedhouses/franklincastle/
Findagrave.com—http://www.findagrave.com/cgi-bin/fg.cgi?
page=gsr&GSiman=1&GScid=645569&GSfn=&GSln=Tiedemann
Ancestry.com—Tiedemann, Hannes
-Delaware:
A Native Ghost by Rae D. Henkle
Ghosts of Historic Delaware, Ohio, John Ciochetty
http://www.greetingsfromdelawareohio.com/delawarecountylandmarks
Haunted Tomb-
Bob Parrott - Union County Historical Society
Suzanne Kienbaum-Reference Assistant, Marysville Public Library
Ancestry.com: John Edwin Robinson
-Franklin:
Ohio Haunted Places: http://ohiohauntedplaces.com/?m=200906
Chimney Rock
ohiogenealogyexpress.com/gallia/galliaco_bios_s.htm#sheltonClaiborn
http://archiver.rootsweb.ancestry.com/th/read/VAPITTSY/2000-
07/0964575419
 Citations: Collection of family histories from Gallia Co in 1980) From History of
Gallia Co. Ohio by W Grody
-Greene:
History of Greene County, Ohio: Its People, Industries and Institutions Volume 1-
By Michael A. Broadstone
History of Greene County, Together with Notes on the Northwest and the State of
Ohio: RS Dills
Ancestry.com: 1870 and 1880 census for Yellow Springs
http://freepages.genealogy.rootsweb.ancestry.com/~gen2/news.htm
http://www.findagrave.com/cgi-bin/fg.cgi?
page=pv&GRid=14988999&PIpi=3602735
-Hardin County:
Hardin Armory:
Findagrave.com
Hardin County: By Ronald I. Marvin Jr.
--Jefferson:
Panhandle Bridge: http://www.trainlife.com/albums/photo/view/
album_id/3724/photo_id/309954
-Knox
History of Knox County, Ohio: Its Past and Present, Containing a Condensed
 By Albert Adams Graham
http://ww2.ohiohistory.org/etcetera/exhibits/swio/pages/
content/1913_flood.htm
-Historical information on Knox County: James K. Gibson, Director Knox County
Historical Society Museum
Jim Linkous- Knox Times: knoxtime.com/
-Lucas County
Oliver House: http://theoliverhousetoledo.com/history.html
Toledo-Lucas County Library—staff interview
-Madison County
Red Brick Tavern: files.usgwarchives.net/pa/berks/history/family/tall0003.txt
http://historicredbricktavern.com/
-Mahoning
Jacksonville Illinois Newspaper, Sunday morning August 21, 1949 'Ghost' In Ohio
Town Draws Many People Each Night
-Montgomery
Bessie Little
http://www.daytonhistorybooks.com/bessielittleyoung.html
http://www.daytonhistorybooks.com/albert_frantz.html
Rock Island Argus., September 07, 1896, Page 6, Image 6
The Valentine Democrat., September 10, 1896, Image 2 2nd
Courthouse:
http://www.greaterdaytonregion.com/2011/03/29/history-bit-the-old-
courthouse/
http://www.mcohio.org/services/communications/mcreport/index.html
Frances Dick Hanging: http://www.daytonhistorybooks.com/page/
page/2985104.htm
http://www.daytonhistorybooks.com/manhangedtwice.html
James Murphy Hanging: The Highland weekly news., August 31, 1876

Harry Adams: http://www.mcohio.org/Sheriff/jail_info.cfm
Dayton Daily News:
Daily Republican Register April 28, 1988, Mount Carmel, Illinois
Syracuse Post Standard April 28, 1988
Haunted Dayton: Ghost Stories of The Gem City Frank H. Coleman Jr
Long Gone Graveyard:
daytonhistorybooks.com/sullivancemeteries.html
Historic Maps
Third Street (McAfee) **Ghost**
Candler Kinfok --John M'affee Trial and Hanging
http://www.daytonhistorybooks.com/page/page/2985041.htm
www.dayton.va.gov
Victoria Theatre:
Putnam County District Library
Patterson Castle:
(Xenia) Daily Gazette Thursday, May 18, 1967.
Germantown Cemetery:
Photo Soldier: Library of Congress Prints LC-DIG-ppmsca-35625
Library Park Ghost: © Raisa Kanareva - Fotolia.com
-Morgan County:
www.ohgen.net/ohmorgan/brick.htm
Morgan County Historical Society
Morgan County Courthouse:
Strange Nemesis Following Case: Perrysburg journal., October 28, 1910, Pg 3
Worry Cause of Tragedy:The Bemidji Daily Pioneer., October 06, 1909
Officer Shot by Crazy Man: Omaha daily bee., September 08, 1905
Morgan County Historical Society
Theresa's Haunted History of the Tri-State
-Muskingum
Haunted Places: The National Directory: Ghostly Abodes, Sacred Sites, UFO ... By
Dennis William Hauck
Stumpy's Hollow:
The Ohio Guide By Federal Writers' Project, Writers' Program (Ohio)
The Times Recorder, Zanesville, Ohio Thursday 2 October 1947
-Pickaway County
http://stagespondnaturepreserve.info/Local_Lore_Information.htm
http://www.ohiohistorycentral.org/w/Circleville,_Ohio?rec=686
-Pike
Hewitt:
http://www.rootsweb.ancestry.com/~ohpcgs/pictures/id220.htm
http://www.waverlyinfo.com/page/6009/Waverly-Pg-Hist-Pa
Jim Henry, Author Pike's Past—The Pike County News Watchman,
January 2006
Historical collections of Ohio : an encyclopedia of the state : history both general
and local, geography, with descriptions of
-Putnam
http://www.hancockparks.com/ThingsToDo/ScenicByway/PointsofInterest.aspx
-Richland
http://www.examiner.com/article/bissman-building-not-all-employees-left-at-
the-end-of-their-shift
Women's Club:
Hedges also was an early Mansfield historian by Peggy Mershon
Renaissance Theatre: The Mansfield News Publication: 11 Oct 1932 - Mansfield,
The Mansfield News Publication: 11 Oct 1932 - Mansfield, Ohio
Victim Tells Story of Famous Shooting- Marguerite Miller, Mansfield News-Journal,
January 12, 1951
Theatre Man Shot During Mystery Movie - Marguerite Miller January 11, 1951
-Warren:
McClung Murder:
http://www.rootsweb.ancestry.com/~ohwarren/Bogan/bogan047.htm
Marietta daily leader., June 29, 1901, Image 2
Butler County Democrat:Thursday April 18, 1901
rootsweb.ancestry.com/~ohwarren/Cemetery/Dogstreet/dogstreet.htm
Powder Plant: http://www3.gendisasters.com/ohio/2326/kings-station%2C-oh-
railroad-car-explosion%2C-jul-1890
Golden Lamb:
http://www.goldenlamb.com/pages/history/default/3/